CONTENTS

Giving Back
About The Author

This book is dedicated to so many people.

To my parents and husband for being so supportive and encouraging.

To the Cuyahoga county library for having an amazing writing workshop that got me back into the swing of things. They also have an amazing advanced writing workshop that let me workshop this book (Thank you Ursula, Gary, Kathie, and Correne).

To Kim Coyle for being an amazing student teacher for my high school senior English class. Had she not allowed us to create short stories with vocab words, Leza would have never been create.

And to the readers. Thank you for taking the time to enjoy a piece of my heart and soul.

LEZA OF THE ALPHA LINE

by Rachael Balke

CHAPTER 1

The sun foretold death, as did the summons of war, but the crimson sun sent goose bumps up my arms as it crested the horizon, prickling the fine hairs that grew there.

I had made up my mind that previous night; I didn't need my parents' permission to go fight. My pack practically considered me an adult as my first change had occurred nearly three years ago. Regardless, my parents were having a hard time accepting that fact, especially given the current circumstances.

"You're seventeen, Leza!" my mother cried as if I had forgotten.

"Precisely!" I clipped back. "Marzi, Jerico, and Presly are all going. They're all seventeen as well."

"Those pups are not my only daughter!" Mother's voice crept up in a shrill. Her sienna skin flushed red with anger.

"This is not an ordinary skirmish. It's not just another pack venturing onto our hunting grounds. They will fight this to the death." Father responded with a calmer tone, but he spoke to me as if I were a child. As if I didn't understand the finality of death.

I balled my hands into fists to keep myself from striking out in anger. "All the more reason to defend my home!"

Mother opened her mouth to say something, but I walked out before she could utter a word. I would not sit around and let other pack members defend me. I am more than capable of taking care of myself.

Mother was up and stationed on her porch to ensure I followed their rules. I hid in shame while my uncle, Head Alpha, led our people off to battle and glowered at Mother as soon as he had passed. Sure, not everyone was going. Some stayed to take care of the young. Others stayed to tend to a small bit of farming. I had no legitimate reason to stay behind, and it pained me to watch them go.

◆ ◆ ◆

Seconds felt like hours, standing there in a silent showdown with my mother. We set our faces with equal amounts of determination. The sun inched its way higher into the sky.

Fortunately, after an hour had legitimately passed, Mother got called away, which put an end to our stalemate. She is the pack's healer, and someone's pup wasn't feeling well.
I jumped at this opportunity and ran as fast as I could in the

direction that Uncle had set off toward earlier. I prayed I would get there in time to be of some assistance. Everyone else had also traveled on foot, but I felt so far behind. Running on two legs felt so slow compared to the speed I can reach on four, but the full moon passed nights ago. I wouldn't be able to feel that power again for another month. In the meantime, I would just have to rely on these two well-toned legs. I bounded over a twisted root that sought to catch my bare feet mid-stride. Greens and browns melted together as I beat my way through the territory.

◆ ◆ ◆

My heartbeat rose to a level it had never beaten before. Excitement and terror warred with each other inside of me, excitement to flex my skills and show off all I've learned; terror at the prospect of greeting death or losing those close to me.

Packs don't fight to the death. The only time a fight to the death can occur is when another pack member directly challenges the Head Alpha. We keep to ourselves, but today we're coming to the aid of a sister pack defending themselves from an attack by The Appointed.

The Appointed is a group that consists of a variety of supernatural beings. Their primary principle is that they believe it is "unjust" to be "confined" to the island that we all call home. Nothing is confining us to this island. We can travel to the mainlands anytime we wish, and any supernatural being is welcome to move and establish roots here.

Until now, The Appointed were just a group of disgruntled beings spouting fantastical ideas about overpowering the humans and taking over the mainlands. They seem to have forgotten the bloodshed our ancestors faced; human fear of things they cannot comprehend nearly wiped all of us out. According to the stories passed down, human fear is so potent they often turn on their own people simply due to their different colors of skin.

Before, The Appointed would wander into villages and spew their vile propaganda in an attempt to rally more to their cause, but now they have become violent.

They've begun waging full-on attacks in retaliation to any place that runs them out of town, which has caused problems for those of us who view The Appointed as crazy and gladly welcome the idea of living out our lives in the sanctuary the Four Mothers gave us.

The Four Mothers were powerful witches who combined their powers to provide a sanctuary for supernatural beings. The Americas had proven to be just as dangerous as the old world, with the witch hunts beginning in 1645, but the witches weren't the only beings facing extinction. In response, The Four Mothers extended their blessing to any creature that wanted it. Generations have prospered here, but now The Appointed threatened nearly 400 years of relative peace.

Sure, us werewolves can fight among ourselves, but life on the island means we can live without constant fear, always having to keep our guard up. Our children can play outside without fear of kidnapping and death. All but The Appointed agree that this is a privileged life.

We have maintained relative peace because each supernatural species has formed their own secluded, tight-knit communities, but that doesn't mean we never interact with each other. Traders make their living by peddling to different settlements.

Werewolves inhabit the middle section of the island, giving us plenty of room to hunt. Witches live in the northeast and shapeshifters stay in the northwest. Very few vampires left the mainlands when the Four Mothers offered them this gift, fearing the food scarcity island life would challenge them with. The few that live here inhabit the mountains, relying on human traffickers to smuggle them food. Not all interactions with smugglers are as gruesome, though. They bring the communities clothing, fabric, food, and trinkets from time to time.

I love this land. It is my home, and I consider protecting it and all beings that live here a privilege.

◆ ◆ ◆

The coppery smell of blood caught my attention. I must be getting closer.

The trees thinned, and I burst out onto the open field. Gore met my eyes. I saw bodies strewn lifelessly across the ground, their insides torn out. Red puddles stained the ground, and the grass stood at various heights, disturbed by the struggle.

I didn't notice someone had targeted me until he seemingly materialized before me. Either he was incredibly fast or I hadn't focused enough on my surroundings. Both possibilities frightened me.

Chestnut hair stood out in contrast to his pale, grey skin. A sharp chin, defined cheekbones, and an upturned nose gave him a snobby appearance, but his red eyes reflected sadistic pleasure.

A vampire? In daylight? That shouldn't be possible.

He grinned, exposing his finely pointed fangs, but as he did so, a ripple danced across his cheeks. An enchantment, something protecting him.

" La fillette!" He exclaimed with enjoyment. "It is too dangerous here for you." His eyes swept over me with a pang of hunger. "Pitié, beauty must die here."

My breath caught in my chest. Have I trained enough for this? Am I ready? I didn't have an instructor this time to stop things from turning too rowdy. What if I make a mistake?

I pushed everything from my mind to avoid any further distractions and straightened my back to stand taller. Despite pivoting my right foot behind me to obtain a more balanced and defensive stance, the vampire's hands darted out and shoved me, breaking my form instantly.

My body landed with a slight splash in a puddle of something dark and sticky.

He licked his lips and moved to stand over me. The ground made a squishing noise as I scrambled backward, away from him.

The devilish grin never left his face as he continued slowly advancing on me with a mixture of confidence and arrogance.

As I shuffled backward, I almost yelped when I bumped against something, but it was just a tree. I used its trunk to get back on my feet, and the rough bark scraped at my palms.

He had closed the distance between us during the short time I had looked back. Something moved toward my head, and I barely ducked in time, resulting in the vampire's hand shooting into the tree trunk.

Luckily, he couldn't free his hand immediately, so I balled up my fist and landed a hard punch to his jaw.

Angered, he slashed out with his free hand. I jumped to the right and looked down as I heard a tearing noise. One of his long fingernails caught the front of my shirt, ripping it horizontally. A red line of blood appeared on my stomach.

Before I could get out of his way, his hand shot up and grabbed onto my left bicep with an iron grip.

The vampire moved his face closer to my body and inhaled deeply. "Ah." He sighed as if he had just smelt the sweetest bouquet. "Délicieuse."

He yanked his hand free from the tree, and my eyes widened in terror. *I don't want to die here!*

My foot shifted back as I struggled in his grip and landed on a pointy rock. In a panic, I used my toes to maneuver it from the ground and flung it up into my free hand.

Without thinking, I reared back and struck him in the temple. Unnaturally dark blood coated the tip of my improvised weapon, and I reared back for another strike.

He caught my wrist mid-strike and squeezed it so hard the pain forced me to drop the rock.

He issued a light-hearted laugh, let go of my hand, and grabbed my neck. I tried to jerk away, but he tightened his grip, keeping me there. Every breath I took felt shallower than the last.

His cheeks pulled back into a big smile, and he opened his mouth wide. The ripple danced again, but this time it looked thinner than before. He froze, then let go of my arm. He waved his fingers around to catch the light. His brows furrowed.

He looked back at me with disappointment in his eyes, then back at his fingers.

An audible sound of frustration followed as he uncurled his fingers from my neck.

"Some other time." He promised, then retreated into the woods.

I crumpled to the ground, coughing and gasping for air.

◆ ◆ ◆

"Leza?" a gruff voice rang out. A man came trotting over to me. He wasn't caked in blood or covered in wounds like you would expect someone to be leaving a battlefield. He almost looked too clean. His mussed, cropped blond hair revealed some struggle, but he didn't have the grime one would expect from being thrown around. His jaw looked firmly set as he approached me.

I scrambled to my feet as I recognized the voice belonged to my uncle.

I straightened my back and tried not to wince. With the danger gone, I started to feel all my injuries.

"Are you hurt?" He asked. His eyes moved toward the bruised handprints forming clearly on my neck and bicep.

Hurt? I was lucky to be alive, but I couldn't let Uncle know how terribly unprepared I had been for battle. I assumed he hadn't witnessed my battle. If he had, I'm sure he would have greeted me in a much different manner.

"I'll be ok," I replied. I couldn't bear the thought of disappointing Uncle; I've looked up to him my whole life and have been lucky enough to train with him.

"Good," He nodded. "Don't I explicitly recall your mother forbidding you from coming?"

Great, a lecture.

"I'm seventeen, I am old enough to help when-"

He cut me off with a laugh. "I'll be sure to put in a good word for you. Maybe that brother of mine can make sure you don't get into too much trouble."

"Dad? Against mom? No way. She'll have my hide for sure."

Uncle laughed some more. "Come," He said, clasping an arm around my shoulders. "Let's go home."

I nodded in agreement and began walking with him; home sounded fantastic right now.

"You'll have at least a few hours to say goodbye to your hide. I need your father's counsel when we get back and," He took a moment to glance behind us at the wounded, either supported by friends or being pulled along on makeshift litters. His expression dimmed as a somber look took over his face. "Your mother will have her hands full."

CHAPTER 2

The Vampire

Trees passed by only as blurs of brown bark as his feet deftly avoided rocks, foliage, and upturned roots.

"Zut! I need to find shelter, immédiatement!"

With each passing second, the protection faded. André glanced at his fingers. They practically pulsated as the charm struggled to protect him from exposure. Was it his imagination, or could he feel heat building at the back of his neck?

His eyes darted around, and he could feel the beginnings of panic trying to take hold of his mind.

There!

A cedar, more like three cedar trees, inoculated together to form one giant tree, would be his savior today. The trunk appeared at least four times his circumference. Halfway up the tree sat a hollow just big enough for André to squeeze into, and with leaves thick enough to block the sunlight. It looked dodgy but good enough in the pinch he found himself in.

André made a break for it with all the speed he possessed. He clutched the trunk so hard that in his haste his fingers left holes in the bark as he climbed.

For a moment, he thought he had misjudged the hollow, and he that would not fit.

"Dieu vous damne, allez!" He shrieked while trying to maneuver himself inside. The bark scratched at his face as he entered. The small space pinned his knees uncomfortably close to his chest, but at least he shouldn't burn now.

Flashing eyes caught his attention. André's trespassing had pinned the hollow's occupant, a big barred owl, to the other side of the small space. André snarled at it, and the owl raised a taloned foot in response, ready to lash out. His hand shot out and grabbed the bird by the neck, silencing its shrieks.

"It's all her little bird's fault I am out here."

André brought the owl to his mouth, not particularly hungry, but thirsty for a kill nonetheless. He sank his fangs into the meaty part of the owl's chest as it struggled feebly in his grasp.

Once the creature's heart gave its last thu-bump, André pulled his head away, and a dark trickle of blood ran down his chin.

"I was once one of her little pets, too, you know?" He told the limp, lifeless owl. " In my foolishness, I actually believed we were more than that." André paused. Remembering how close he had once felt to her. After Maria, he didn't think he could ever feel close to another woman. Which left his current circumstance with an even nastier taste in his mouth. His eyes darkened. "We had such grand plans in the beginning. Her bloodlust seemed to almost match mine." He gave a humorless chuckle. "But now look at me. Talking to the corpse of a bird in a paumé tree!" He flung the corpse out of the hallow.

André shifted his body in an attempt to get into the most comfortable position, but was unsuccessful.

"We were supposed to topple the filthy humans from their pedestal, avenge all our brethren… avenge my Maria.

◆ ◆ ◆

I was a fool for insisting we stay in France. I was young and drunk on my new immortality. She was older and more experienced; I should have listened, but I thought if we were careful with our meals, then no one would ever suspect a thing. We could stay and enjoy the opera houses, we could have the latest fashion, we could have it all. And we did, for a short while. I still don't know what gave us away. What suspicious crumb we left behind.

Our château was in the countryside with no neighbors to speak of. Maria paid her servants handsomely to ignore any odd requests. We never took meals back to our home. We attended parties to stay in good standing with the community and never dined on the aristocracy. No one should have been none the wiser, yet somehow someone still found us out.

We had gone to bed, like any other day. Dark velvet curtains drawn over the windows provided us with security from the daylight. A matching set of curtains hung around our four-post bed added a second layer of privacy. Maria slept naked, snuggled into the crook of my arm. Our bodies fit together perfectly.

In the midst of our deep slumber, Maria was pulled from my embrace. At first, she didn't even wake up. A man dragged her by the ankles and bounded her hands with a rosary before she could gather her bearings. Pulled so quickly and violently from sleep, I couldn't react fast enough before the man ripped down a curtain and bathed the space between us in sunlight. He muttered something I couldn't understand, but I recognized the language as Turkish. Smoke rose from her bound hands.

A maid burst into the room with a flintlock in her hands. The man, unphased, grinned as he shoved Maria into the light. The gun went off, but it was too late. Maria's agonized shrieks filled the room.

◆ ◆ ◆

"Majie seems more content with playing warlord each year."
André let his natural instincts take over and slept.

CHAPTER 3

Leza

The journey back home didn't feel as long as I had expected it to. My fight was brief, but it completely exhausted me. Uncle instructed me to walk at the head of the pack with him, which made the journey better. The sun hung just past midday when the outskirts of our village came into view.

"Home."

We had long spotted the great Velcome mountain before arriving back at our village, situated at its base. We've claimed ownership of this land since the blessed migration. A lot of my battle companions looked worn. Some would head to my mother for care. Others stopped at the small river that flows through the middle of the village to wash the signs of battle off themselves. My face scrunched as I thought about how cold that water must be before shaking my head. I intended to make my way to our bathing springs, only a short hike up the mountain, to clean myself. Feeling the waves of pain from my battle echoing throughout my body as I moved, I figured a hot bath would help soothe my wounds.

As I approached her hut, I braced for the screeches that would echo throughout the entire village, but the house greeted me with nothing but silence. My mother wasn't home. Had she been home, she would have emerged with rage in the likes of which the village had never seen before. I knew the battle brought enough wounded to keep her busy at some temporary nursing station rather than waiting at home ready to scold me, but I was in for it when she got back.
Having delivered me safely back home, Uncle started walking in the other direction. "I'm going to hold a meeting," Uncle said. "I want to get the wisdom of The Council, and I'd like to hear from the pack as well. Tell your parents if you see them." I nodded, and Uncle continued on his way.

◆ ◆ ◆

I rounded the corner and approached my own hut. Last year, as my sixteenth birthday present, my parents built me a place just for myself.

It's nothing grand. Just a one-room rounded structure, measuring twelve by fourteen feet.

I never understood the point of wearing shoes so before entering, I stopped to wash my feet in the bowl of water I keep by my front door. I scrubbed at them until I made sure I would not track anything in. As I passed through the threshold, I looked toward the right side of the room, longing for my loft bed. I dreaded having to climb up into it later. Rest sounded great right now, but I had to clean up first. I trudged my way over, making sure to give the decorative cushions on the floor a wide berth. I didn't want to think about cleaning them for the next time I had guests over. Instead of lugging myself into the bed, I pulled out a fresh pair of clothes and a towel from the dresser beneath the loft.

Eager to go to the springs, I turned my tired body to the chest that lived on the opposite wall, again side stepping the cushions and passing by my hearth on the back wall. I heaved the lid open and ran a hand over a rack storing several transparent vials. Each vial was filled with a thick, syrup-like substance, but each one had its own unique color. I selected the warm honey color and the one colored a deep purple. I removed the vial compartment and made a quick grab for my bar of soap. Now that I had all of my supplies, I was ready to head for the springs.

◆ ◆ ◆

With every reluctant stride, my muscles grumbled in complaint. I had never been so thankful that my hut sat rather close to the base of the mountain.
It didn't take long until I could hear the rumbling of the waterfall. Although thin, it pours from somewhere higher up the mountain and feeds the springs. In order to keep our bathing springs clean, my pack had long ago dug channels to concentrate the wastewater runoff, allowing the filth to be carried off by an artificial creek.

I had my pick of the pools when I reached my destination. Everyone else must have been too eager about the council meeting and settled for a quick wash in the village river.

Uncle and I hadn't exchanged many words on the way home earlier, but he informed me that the enemy had retreated. It struck me as odd and uncharacteristically democratic for Uncle to consult the pack before deciding on our next move, but if we decide to go after them, we should first make sure we have the numbers to win.

Not like they'd need my opinion, anyway. I thought to myself as I made my way over toward the biggest and the deepest pool located higher than the rest. The water sat at a comfortable chest level for me when I stood in the center, and seeing it unoccupied was rare.

I set my things down at the edge of the pool and uncorked the deep-purple-colored vial. Using only four drops, I established a perimeter. A faint sizzling sound rose as the drops hit the ground. A thick, grey smoke veil inked its way from the ground and rose about six feet in the air. It then stretched out and connected with the other drops, forming a privacy screen for my bath.

I corked the vial, then retrieved the next one, pouring a thin, goopy, honey-colored stream into the pool. It started slowly, at first, but the water rapidly bubbled like a pot of water over a fire. Steam rose and warmed the surrounding air.
The blood that caked my ruined clothes made it difficult to peel them off as the cloth stuck firmly to my flesh and pulled at the little hairs on my body. I took a moment to assess the damage my clothes had taken. Along with being bloody, my battle had tattered my pants at the knees, and my shirt had several slashes in it. I don't think they would ever be wearable again; still, I carefully folded them and set them aside far away from my clean pair. A token of my first real fight.
Before stepping in, I poked a toe in the water. A sigh of relief left me as my toe discovered the temperature to be perfect, not too hot. The rest of my body slid in soon after, and I made my way toward the center of the pool where I sat on the bottom for a few moments, submerging everything. Once I resurfaced, I took inventory of my injuries. My stomach had a shallow cut that ran across it, long, but not serious. It will practically heal by tomorrow afternoon. The bruises are what I expected to take a few days to disappear. The handprint on my arm left by the filthy vampire's intense grip looked black, blue, and purple, all blotting up and mingling together. I assumed the one on my neck likely looked similar. Even the lightest of touches as I brushed my fingertips on the middle of my neck forced an involuntary wince.

I cursed myself for not bringing a hand mirror and rolled my eyes; no way is this going to go unnoticed by my mother.

I took a deep breath, centering myself, and mentally checked in with the rest of my body. Almost every muscle in my body felt sore.

My hair needed to be washed three separate times before all the dirt and blood allowed it to return to its natural shade of sand. Once clean, my head felt so much lighter. I made slow work of washing my body, not only did I feel sore, but the effort I had to put into cleaning my hair didn't help my muscles. While the hot water did wonders for them, I wanted to avoid upsetting them any further.

I allowed myself to linger a bit longer before pulling myself out of the pool. Almost immediately, the bubbles slowed, and by the time I had toweled off, the water stood completely still. After I finished getting dressed and exited my smoke screen, the smoke rose and dissipated.

I stared up at it, transfixed by its disappearing wisps. The sound of footsteps caught my attention and brought me back to earth. It startled me because I didn't expect anyone else to come to the springs right now. People commonly mingle after council meetings. While the meetings themselves are frequently short, people can spend a fair amount of time gossiping afterward. That, and I think the glory hounds like to stay blood-soaked so others can marvel at their bravery. Soon, I should start developing a presence at The Council since I have aspirations of one day serving as an elite member of the pack, but for now, I trust my uncle to do what's best for all of us.

◆ ◆ ◆

"Hello, Little Alpha." A smooth voice called.

I rolled my eyes. I hated being called that. Not only was it stupid, but most of the time, it just sounded like people were mocking me.

I looked around to locate my uninvited company and noticed a man leaning against a nearby rock face. The voice belonged to Deegan. If you just took Deegan at face value, he seemed a very appealing creature. Thick, tousled brown hair, dark chocolate eyes, tall, and extremely fit and muscular. You'd almost call him a dreamboat until you hung around him for more than two seconds. He was uncomfortably flirtatious toward someone eight years his junior, and that just didn't sit right with me. Every other girl in the pack would drool all over herself if he showed them as much attention as I get. Truthfully, I think he's convinced himself that he can elevate his position in the pack if won me over. True, a strong partner can provide you with strong children, but that doesn't give you strength. I also wonder how much of his displayed attraction stems from my disinterest in him. Maybe he's just fixating on something he can't have.

"Deegan." I acknowledged, before fixing my attention on making sure I grabbed everything. No one likes a litterer. I noticed Deegan wore his chest bare, save for dried blood and scratches. Blood also matted his hair and soaked his shorts. Of course, he would have only gone to the Shilo pack's aid for nothing other than the glory that came with it.

Deegan jumped into the nearest pool and scrubbed away the dried brown blood under its waterfall.

"The Council still hasn't made a decision." He informed me casually as I passed by.

Baffled, I stopped in my tracks. "Still?! Almost a full hour has passed since we returned home! Uncle should be enforcing some plan of action by now!"

"Looks like he wants to get as many opinions as he can this time." Deegan pulled himself out of the pool despite still having spots of blood in his hair. As he approached, he combed his fingers through his wet hair. He stood a bit too close to me. "The meeting is going to last a while."

I released a sigh of exhaustion. "I need rest," I admitted. The battle taxed me physically and mentally. I reassured myself that I simply felt too drained to understand Uncle's intentions. There had to be a reason I couldn't immediately identify. He's never needed input from the entire pack before. Sure, he's surveyed the feel of the pack before, but he's never needed *everyone's* input. To make the situation worse, the decision seemed painfully obvious. We go after The Appointed and make them pay.

"Yeah, I noticed you managed to catch up with the rest of us. It was..." He searched for the word. "Invigorating, right?" He grinned. This grin could melt the heart of any lady pack member, and I hate to admit it, but my guard dropped a little.

"It sure was something," I said. Before he could say anything else, I turned and made my way down the mountain toward my hut.

◆ ◆ ◆

Once finally settled back at home, I barely had enough time to pull the covers over my head before sleep claimed me.

CHAPTER 4

A vigorous knock at the door woke me from my slumber. My eyes fluttered, struggling against staying open. I pulled the covers back up to my chin when the knock came again. "Coming." I groaned. My bed provided warmth and comfort, pressuring me to stay. Reluctantly, I forced the covers off of me and untangled my legs from its cozy grasp. Still struggling to commit fully to getting up, I laid there a moment longer, and there followed another knock. "I'm coming!"

I sat up and dangled my legs over the edge of my bed, taking a moment to release a yawn so big my jaw popped and stretched my arms as high as my sore muscles would let me. No light streamed in from outside, leaving my hut in complete darkness. The moon had not yet gathered enough strength to produce much light. I hopped down and hurried over to light a fire in my hearth. The light didn't illuminate the room well enough, so I dug out a vial containing sunshine-colored liquid from my rack. I made a mental note to haul in more firewood from my parents' stack soon. As soon as the drop touched a finger of the flame, the light intensified, illuminating the entire room.

After returning the vial, I took a quick peek in the mirror and hurriedly made an attempt to look less disheveled. When I finally went to open the door, I felt a tinge of embarrassment about how much time had passed.

"Good evening, Little Alpha." Greeted me as the door swung open.

"Deegan?" I yawned. He leaned against the left post in a cool, unbothered manner with a lantern propped up on one of my railings. He still hadn't put on a shirt, but at least he had on a clean pair of shorts. "What are you doing here?"

"Head Alpha requests you come to The Council meeting."

"That's still going on?" I asked, baffled. Deegan only nodded. This *was* out of the ordinary. Never in my life had a council meeting *ever* lasted this long. What time was it even? I looked past the glow of the lantern and confirmed that it had to at least be eleven o'clock at night. We got back around two o'clock, so that meant this council meeting had been running for at least nine hours.

Deegan waited outside by the door while I kicked the fire out. He let me take my time without interruption.

"Shall we?" He asked as darkness returned to the hut.

Deegan cocked an eyebrow at me, and I nodded. We started walking, but the silence felt too awkward. "What's happened? Council meetings never last all day."

"It hasn't. The discussion lasted most of the afternoon, then Head Alpha declared a break so people could clean up and rest. He said something about "not wanting people's minds being clouded with war." Deegan shrugged and gave me a pointed look. I couldn't read his expression, so we walked the rest of the way in silence.

◆ ◆ ◆

You can't miss the Council building. It has more than enough room to house two packs under its roof. While it's not very common, occasionally Head Alphas from other packs venture over to hold an audience with our Alpha to either ask for protection or to redefine the pack's hunting grounds. When that happens, the visiting pack brings a large majority of their people along for the meeting.

Uncle already sat centered in the Head Alpha throne-like seat, elevated above the rest, when I entered the building. I pictured myself in that chair one day as my eyes brushed over its mahogany wood, appreciating its elegant craftsmanship and high back that finished with a curl at the top. The back of the chair depicted each phase of the moon, starting with the new moon at the bottom and ending with the full moon centered behind Head Alpha's head. Each armrest ended with a magnificently sculpted wolf's head carved with such detail it looked as if they could morph out of the chair. At a glance, one may assume such a solid wooden chair would lack comfort, but a plush, dark-red cushion remedied this issue.

A good-sized crowd had re-formed, and all eight Council Elders sat ready to continue, their seats flanking my Uncle's. I weaved my way through the crowd to get situated toward the front. I had just elbowed my way there when Uncle spotted me and motioned for me to approach him. As I made my way up, I noted my father seated behind Uncle in the section reserved for people Head Alpha trusts, which typically consists of family members and the occasional close friend.

"Leza." The men said at the same time. My father sounded surprised while my uncle casually issued a greeting.

"Father." I leaned in and gave him a quick hug. Father's embrace always felt warm and reassuring.

"Uncle," I greeted, and bowed respectfully.

He laughed and gestured to the seat behind him on his left. "Sit." He chuckled.

My father and I exchanged glances. This was new. Uncle had never asked me to sit behind him before. I tried to keep the cockiness out of my expression. Aside from Head Alpha and the Council Elders, this was the only other seating in the building.

Uncle cleared his throat, and the murmurings from the crowd fell silent.

"This morning we faced a terrible tragedy." His voice boomed through the hall. "We lost more than I would like to admit, and the devastation the Shilo pack suffered is greater than our own."

The crowd shifted uncomfortably. "Go after them!" someone shouted from the back. A small ripple of agreement traveled through the crowd, but only in quiet mumbles.

Uncle motioned for silence. "No one is disputing this morning's tragedy, but too much time has passed since the attack; would it be wise to go after them now?"

Everything seemed to fall into a vacuum and move in slow motion. Why wouldn't he want to track them down and ensure they can't bother us again? I looked over at my uncle. His lips still moved as he continued to address the crowd, but I wasn't hearing a word he said. Red boiled up in my vision.

"What?!" I leaped from my chair, unable to hold my outburst any longer.

The closest Elder member grumbled at me, but Uncle raised a hand, silencing him. "Continue, Leza."

"You were there, Uncle. You saw what they did to our sister pack. You witnessed firsthand what they did to us. How long do you think it'll be before they strike again? They may even target us next."

Uncle watched me, his expression unbothered as if we were just arguing if roasted rabbit or deer made for a better feast.

I wheeled around to face the crowd. "Do you want to see our home destroyed? Ransacked? Your neighbors dead?" The crowd had stood still during my initial outburst, shocked, but now as I spoke, they shook their heads. I turned back to face my uncle. "The Appointed have plagued this island for far too long, and I, for one, am sick of them!"

My father's jaw dropped. Many people carried different expressions in response to my blatant show of disrespect. I didn't want to push it too far, so I finished my point and sat back down.

The crowd blinked in astonishment. Deegan stood several rows back, and his expression revealed he wholeheartedly agreed. His eyes, however, conveyed a deeper emotion I didn't want to entertain.

"So, what do you propose we do?" Uncle asked.

I gaped at him. I just clearly stated what I thought we should do. Confused by his blatant lack of understanding, I replied, "You're Head Alpha here, Uncle. You know what's best for the pack."

He relaxed further back in this throne, contemplating. After a painfully long pause, the crowd erupted. Of course, Deegan started, followed shortly by others.

The Elders shouted, calling for order in a round-robin fashion, issuing one before the final syllable of the last. The room plunged into confusion. Uncle just sat there with a perplexed expression that didn't quite look genuine. He clearly knew the wishes of his people, but he wasn't taking action. He just sat there and listened to the crowd cry. We still had time to catch the retreated enemies' trail, but if we waited much longer, we'd lose that opportunity. Even the most skilled trackers would like Uncle to give them a vague idea of which direction to follow.

My uncle's eyes scanned the crowd. I wanted to shake him and demand to know what he was thinking, but instead, I quietly got up from my seat, snuck to the nearest wall, and slipped through the crowd out of the building. If anyone noticed, they didn't make a scene about it.

After letting my eyes adjust to the surrounding darkness, I stalked off back toward my hut. I didn't want to linger long in case anyone came out after me. I had a choice to make. Do what I feel is right or wait for my Alpha's command.

◆ ◆ ◆

By the time I made it back to my hut, I had already decided. Ensuring our safety from the Appointed was the right thing to do.

I lit a small lantern I kept hanging on the wall, pulled out a travel bag from the depths of my trunk, and began packing clothes and an assortment of vials. I tightly rolled up my sleeping mat, folded a throw blanket to take up as least space as possible, and grabbed my smallest pillow to shove into the pack.

For my provisions, I grabbed four canteens and a handful of handkerchiefs before sneaking over to my parents' shed where they housed bread, dried meats, and large jugs of fresh drinking water.

I maneuvered my new improvised food bags into the backpack after filling all my canteens with water. Getting creative, I crammed hygiene items into the pack.

I mentally checked off all the items I needed and slung the pack onto my shoulders. Before heading out, I grabbed the lantern off its hook, then left.

Leading with my lantern, I paused on my porch to make sure the coast was clear. Huts were the only thing I saw. *Good. Everyone must still be verbally hashing it out in the Council Hall.* I thought and set out on my mission. My first objective, get back to the battlefield as quickly as possible.

When I arrived at the battlefield, I didn't have adrenaline fueling me like last time, and without it, I wasn't mentally prepared for how the battlefield would look, or smell even. Dead bodies littered the ground, strewn everywhere. Blood pools had dried, turning the ground sickly brown. I gazed upon the scene, appalled that Uncle had left the bodies of our fallen people out here like this. It felt disrespectful. We should hold a mass funeral as soon as possible so the bodies can return to Mother Earth.

I extinguished my lantern and tied it to a loop hanging from a strap of my bag. My eyes strained momentarily as they adjusted to the dark, but I wanted nothing to give away my position should anything be hanging around.

The scent of decay pierced my nostrils. I wanted to pinch my nose shut, but considering the conditions, I needed to familiarize myself with the awful stink. Vampires should be the easiest to track after a battle since the faintest whiff of death always clung to them. I took three, deliberate and deep inhales and, even though I wanted to gag, committed the scent to memory. As long as I can locate the trail, I should have no problem following it.

I picked a direction and started walking to put the field behind me. That way, I could pick up on the smell that led me to an undead asshole rather than circling me back to the battlefield.

Slowly, I moved around the perimeter of the field, always keeping it behind me. I took my time. We had already wasted enough time deliberating our next move during the council meeting. I couldn't afford to lose a potential trail to impatience and lack of care. With each step, I took deep breaths. It felt like forever before I picked up on a trail. As soon as I found one, I took off my backpack with excitement and rummaged for a vial that contained a cloudy white liquid.

If I had to choose a favorite enchanted concoction, it would be this one. Most potions work the same for everyone, but not this one. This one provides a unique experience to anyone who uses it by taking on the smell of your favorite scent. For one person, it could smell like fish cooking on a fire, a field of wild daisies, or a lover, but for me, the scent smelled of growing corn and a tinge of skunk spray. Only the person using it can smell this potion. Meaning, no one else will smell their favorite scent when it's used nearby, they won't even know anyone has used it at all!

Carefully, I poured one drop, then returned the vial to the top of my pack. It's not *necessarily* cheating, but it's much easier to track a scent that's pleasant to you.

Unfortunately for me, a vampire's scent can be one of the hardest to follow. Things can easily mask it within the environment. It's also much fainter and fades faster than most scents, but I had no other option than to try. Time passed as I found several leads which led to dead-ends and forced me to backtrack, but every time I found a lead, I poured a drop of my favorite potion.

Tracking was never my favorite subject. Honestly, it can get a little boring. I much preferred focusing my attention on combat training and technique. Because of this, I knew I was leaving a noticeable trail of my own, which really frustrated me. A hunter shouldn't make more tracks and noise than the prey.

As I continued my search, I concentrated heavily on making small, deliberate movements. My head snapped to the left, and I took a defensive crouch when I heard a twig snap nearby. The bushes rustled, and my heart rate quickened; I bared my teeth. My snarl turned into a laugh as a little grey rabbit hopped out of the bush.

I straightened up and relaxed. "You scared me, Rabbit!" I chuckled.

The rabbit sat up on its haunches and stared at me. His left ear twitched, and then he darted back into the bush.

I was mid-step when leaves fell on me from above. With my foot still hovering in the air, I looked up and had just enough time to see red eyes before everything went black.

CHAPTER 5

André

The sound of quick rapid heartbeats woke André up. His stomach twisted in hunger, causing him to clench his jaw in pain. He could easily catch a little tweeting bird and satiate his hunger, but he could hear the heartbeat of something larger headed his way. If he patiently waited, he would have a more satisfying meal. The birds in the tree took flight as André worked himself out of the hollow.

First, an arm, then a shoulder. His torso lengthened out of the hollow. His knees felt cramped from being pressed into his chest for so long. Finally, he shimmed the rest of his body from his small sanctuary.

He crept out onto a branch and waited for his prey.

The heartbeat would approach, then ease away, come close again, then veer off.

"Allez!" André's eyebrows furrow in annoyance. Finally, the prey steadily headed in his direction. He could hear the swoosh of warm, rushing blood in its veins. André focused solely on the approaching creature. Nothing else mattered. His mouth salivated thinking of his upcoming meal.

"Just a bit closer." He edged along the branch as far out as he dared.

His muscles tensed and he sprang, almost as silent as a ghost, had it not been for the rustling of the leaves following his departure from the branch.

With his mouth opened wide, he flew toward his prey, glaring into big, staring blue eyes.

His teeth pierced through the delicate flesh, and he gulped deeply.

◆ ◆ ◆

The creature tasted of the sweetest strawberry, and the warmth was arousing. He moaned.

Images flashed in André's mind. A girl with sandy blonde hair, the creature in his arms, Leza was her name.

In his thirst, he didn't even register that the heartbeat belonged to a girl instead of something like a big deer or the like.

He gulped once again and saw a man with the same sandy blonde hair and a woman who matched Leza's blue eyes. Mother and Father. A feeling of love, warmth, security, and home. She called a village at the base of Velcome mountain her home.

With restraint, André lifted his mouth from the girl's neck and licked at the tiny wells springing from the puncture wounds.

The girl had fainted, and she hung limp like a doll. He took a moment to take in the details of her face, and recognition clicked.

"La fillette, what a surprise." He smirked. "You belong to that silly little pack Majie is playing with. What am I to do with you?" He grinned, his lips pulling away from his teeth. "I could kill you." Almost involuntarily, his mouth moved closer to her neck.

He stopped himself. "Or?" A thought occurred to him. Majie had so many new pets these days, maybe he'd bring home a pet for himself. He frowned. "Was I only ever a pet to you?" He mused to himself. Majie had focused on building her forces for so long now; too long. Perhaps he could give her a taste of her own medicine if he brought home a plaything of his own. Something to distract himself with. André smirked, and it was decided. He slung her over one shoulder and ran.

CHAPTER 6

Threw way back home was uneventful and relatively quick, considering the distance he had to cover. Filled with fresh blood, he ran faster than usual with his renewed energy. He arrived back at base camp with an hour and a half to spare until sunrise.

Paces before the camp entrance, André stopped, heaved the girl from his shoulder, and cradled her in his arms.

"*This should turn some heads,*" He thought as he strode into camp, *"if anyone is still awake, that is.*"* He frowned, the first stroke of doubt coloring his mind that his plan might not work after all.

Camp resembled a hive, more than a village. He entered the expansive structure. Shacks were thrown together and connected by hallways and walkthroughs. Some shacks looked more durable looking than others, and some looked put together in haste. This "hive" is where The Appointed operated out of.

◆ ◆ ◆

The wind stirred to his left, disturbed by a figure who had arrived so unnoticed it seemed to have materialized.

"Care to share your snack?" A sultry voice asked. The woman looked pale, as all vampires do, but one could still detect the discernable bronzed hue still visible on her skin. Her down-turned eyes opened wide in astonishment at the morsel in his arms.

"Non," André replied curtly.

The second vampire's eyes hardened, but her body language remained casual. "Oh, come on," she pouted, "You know how hard it can be to get good prey around here." She attempted to step closer.

"This one is mine!" André barred his teeth. "What is your name again?" He asked aloud, absentmindedly. She opened her mouth to reply, but he cut her off. Shaking his head, "It doesn't matter. Now, get lost." He tsked his tongue in annoyance.

The second vampire hissed, but retreated just the same.

"Good," André thought. "At least one person can attest to my pet." He returned to his task of finding Majie.

◆ ◆ ◆

A small amount of light streamed in from scattered windows as André sauntered casually to Majie's chambers. Anyone roaming around right now would see him with the girl.

Majie's chambers were among the most durable looking in the hive of shelters. Thick oak trucks formed the structure, with a door and windows cut into it, giving it a homey look.

André reached for the knob and gave it a twist, receiving no resistance. As always, she had left her door unlocked and unguarded. Majie warded everything, so she had no need for the typical precautions. André confidently swung the door open, but his face fell with great disappointment when he noticed the empty room.

André's eyebrows knitted together. *Is she waiting for me in my chamber*? He wondered to himself. *I didn't return with the others. Could she be worried about me?"*

He closed the door behind him and made his way to his room, only a walkway length away from Majie's. He opened the door, not caring enough to it closed behind him, and descended a long flight of stairs that stopped at the start of a short hallway. A soft glow lit the space as permanently lit torches lined the wall. André flung his door open. In response to the sudden motion, enchanted torches provided his room with light. To his chagrin, his room also sat empty.

An incoherent noise of equal parts rage and disappointment shot from André's throat. He stomped halfway up the stairs before turning around.

"La chienne!" He exclaimed aloud. "I will not go searching for her."

He slammed his chamber door and locked the bolt behind him. After yesterday's close call, he didn't feel like begging for Majie's attention this close to sunrise.

He tossed the stupid girl down at the far side of the room and made for his coffin. He sighed. "*I guess I can't have her running around.*" He pulled a cord down from a decorative curtain that hung on the wall and bound the girl's hands behind her back. As he did so, he noticed how filthy his sleeves looked. André stomped over to an elegant dresser and inspected himself. Dirt soiled most of his clothes along with small rips and plucks from that damn tree hallow.

He angrily stripped and pulled out a pair of fresh clothes. Glancing at his claw-foot tub a few feet behind him, he decided a bath would have to wait until later. He didn't have enough time to go lugging pails of water into the room to fill the tub with the sunrise so close.

With a look of disdain toward the girl, he stomped over to his coffin, swung the door open, and situated himself against the plush velvet. "Éteindre." He commanded as he shut the coffin door, and by his command, the enchanted torches extinguished.

CHAPTER 7

Ever so slowly, shapes formed within André's mind. The ground felt solid, wood by the sound of his footsteps. He knew he was indoors.

A woman stood in his arms. His chin rested on a slim, uncovered shoulder. Her black hair swished in front of his nose as they swayed. He deeply inhaled the scent of her.

Maria.

With building excitement, he pushed back from her to gaze upon her face.

He missed her so much. André hardly ever seemed to dream anymore, and it was a treat to dream of her.

When he gazed upon her face, the joy and excitement in his features disappeared, replaced by horror and shock. Where her eyes, nose, and mouth should have been, he saw only blank skin. The Maria thing wore a frilly, floor-length, off-the-shoulder dress, a replica of the dress Maria wore in the oil paint André kept of her in his chamber.

André recoiled in disgust.

Majie's chuckle echoed around him, and he snarled in response.

"Oh, come now. It's only a tease." The skin on the face stretched and moved where the mouth should have been as Majie spoke.

"Never do this again!" André snapped and kept his gaze from drifting back toward the nightmarish malformed Maria. "Where were you? I looked for you when I got back."

"Around," Majie responded, dodging the question. "I would have known if something unpleasant happened to you."

André scoffed. "Something unpleasant," He spat out the word, "did almost happen to me."

"Almost, but didn't." She dismissed.

"Well, since you've been so distracted lately, I brought back something to keep me occupied." He looked back toward the Maria thing as it cocked its head in interest. André whirled away, enraged. "Will you please cut that out?"

"If I do that, then I could risk waking you up. It's not even mid-day yet; you'd be very cranky tonight."

"I'm already cranky." He grumbled.

Majie chuckled again. "Dear André..." She sighed without completing her sentence.

André's right eye twitched in annoyance.

"Dear?! She calls me dear and tortures me with this vision?! She wasn't even concerned about the danger I had endured on her stupid errand." He gained control of his face and smoothed it out. "Are we almost done here? I'd like to be refreshed for my pet tonight."

"Ah, yes. You mentioned you brought back something. What is it?"

"Une compagne." André smiled coyly.

"Oh." Did she sound pouty? André couldn't tell.

"You know that new plaything of yours? That strong fellow?" She didn't reply. "Well, I really like how you toy with him, so I have his niece."

The Maria thing's hands shot toward André and grabbed by the throat.

"You what?" She didn't shout, but André could pick up on the fire in her voice.

"It's not like I went and picked her up." André choked out. The hands fell away. André rubbed at his neck as he said. "I found her. Wandering around by herself."

The Maria thing snaked a hand up and stroked his cheek, which he recoiled.

"Well then, I need to come pay her a visit then, don't I?"

André opened his mouth to respond, but she cut him off. "Ah, ah, ah. Rest now." The scene whipped away to darkness.

CHAPTER 8

Leza

I woke up in a crumpled heap on an unfamiliar floor as if someone had just tossed me aside like a mound of laundry.

My head was pounding. I went to rub my temples to get some relief, but when I tried, I found someone had tied my hands behind my back, which also explained why my wrists felt irritated.

Something shaggy and soft cushioned the floor below me.

I blinked hard several times. Laggardly, my mind processed the outlines of tangible things in the room within the darkness.

My body felt incredibly weak. It felt like I hadn't moved in hours, and my stomach growled, reminding me I hadn't eaten in a while. I forced myself into a proper sitting position using the hard, immovable object to my left. Even just that amount of movement made my head spin. My feet weren't bound, but attempting to stand didn't seem like a good idea.

The only source of light I saw came from a thin strip at the bottom of a door. I surveyed the room, trying to gather more details of my surroundings.

Less than a foot away from me stood a low table with bottles on it. Dangerously close to the edge perched a squat, rounded bottle. My tongue felt like a heavy, dry sponge as I realized the extent of my thirst.

I moved my tongue around and swallowed hard to produce some saliva; if I found any success, it made no difference to the desert in my mouth.

I extended my legs out in front of me and placed the soles of my feet on the floor. I scooted my body forward through the wobbly room. Something large was to my right. I lost my balance in a wave of dizziness and fell into it. Luckily, it was soft, and it muted the crashing sound my body would have made otherwise. I rested a moment with my face on the fabric, then started making my way toward the table again. When my knees touched the table, I knew I had made it, but the slight impact jostled the bottle a bit. The swishing sound produced by the bottle's contents rang out to me like a siren's call.

Eagerly, I leaned forward but stopped myself before placing my lips on the bottle. I placed my nose above the opening—lucky for me, it had no cap—and sniffed. It smelled like wine. Warm from being left out, but appeared to pose no threat. I kissed the lips of the bottle. Gently, I rocked my hips back to scoot backward and tip the bottle.

Since the bottle was near empty, it took some careful coaxing to get the contents to my lips. I washed down the dregs of whatever wine this container once held over my tongue and greedily gulped it down, thankful for the moisture.

I had just nudged the bottle back upright on the table when footsteps tickled my ear. Adrenaline started flowing through my veins. The footsteps gradually became louder, soft and small but approaching. My heart started beating faster. Ignoring the clutter on the table, I used it to help myself stand up.

A click resonated from the door's direction as the bolt unlocked. By the time the door flung open, I had successfully managed to stand erect. Light flooded the room. While in normal circumstances, I probably would not consider this to be bright, but in this circumstance, it blinded me.

When I opened my eyes, no matter how many times I blinked, I could not eliminate the dark circles floating in my vision.

A woman stood in the doorway. Behind her, a set of stairs ascended to somewhere else.

Frantically, I looked around for another means of escape, not daring to let this woman out of my sight. The left side of my neck stung with the movement. Nothing. No doors and no windows. A deep red decorative curtain with gold ropes and tassels hung to my left. I noticed it was missing one of its ropes.

The rest of the room offered nothing helpful, just a comfortable-looking ornate plush loveseat and an equally ornate low table. That must have been the soft thing I fell into earlier.

My eyes locked onto a portrait of a dark-haired woman which hung by the now-open door. Of course, I couldn't do much with the oil painting canvas itself, but the frame looked sturdy enough to use as a weapon if I could get close enough to break it. I detected movement in my peripheral and focused my full attention back on the room's new occupant.

Something about her set off internal alarm bells. My reaction to her didn't match her appearance. She had a petite frame and stood a good two inches shorter than me; I could have easily bested her in a fight, even with my hands bound. Long, pale, platinum hair hung loosely down to her mid-back and seemed to emit a light of its own, creating an almost angelic halo around her head. Her oval-shaped face even looked sweet, and her blemish-free skin was sepia with golden undertones. The simple floor-length white dress she wore made her look like a full-grown, gorgeous doll.

If it wasn't for her eyes, she could have passed as someone's well-meaning older sister. Two perfectly placed upturned eyes, the color of a raven's wing, screamed with malicious intent.

My internal alarms at the sight of her meant there was no mistaking who this could be: the leader of The Appointed, Majie.

Rumors spread like wildfire, and word had traveled that the most powerful witch to walk the Earth currently led The Appointed. Some whispers claimed she even possessed more power than Goddess Hecate, but I doubted that could be true.

I didn't want to display any fear, but I don't think I succeeded as I continued looking for an escape route.

"What a sordid little mess you are, Leza from the Alpha Line." Her voice served as the second indicator of her true nature, each word she delivered caked in iciness. She kept her body positioned between me and the door.

My eyes widened, and I took a sharp inhale. How did she know my name? My lineage? Fear crept its way up my spine when I noticed the stinging feeling in my neck again. This time, my eyes widened with realization and hatred chased the fear away.

"Someone fed from me!" My eyes quickly swept the room again, and I registered a small alcove that housed a large, dark, walnut coffin decorated with brass inlays.

"Yes. He quite enjoyed it. Feistiness seems to offset the gaminess werewolves tend to have."

"Hag!" I screeched and spat in her general direction. To my delight, I managed to produce a small drop of saliva.

Her eyes blazed with rage, and almost too calmly, she lifted her hand with her palm facing me. I could feel a surge of power as it crossed the room in my direction. It hit me like a ton of bricks in the chest and sent me crashing into the wall behind me. The wall cracked when I connected, and I landed with a hard thud on my side, once again finding myself on the floor.

"Don't be rude." She scolded. I scoffed, but couldn't think of a comeback. I squirmed in my restraints and noticed the rope starting to give way. Without revealing whoever tied me up sucked at tying a knot, I made small, deliberate movements while she kept talking. *I can get out of this*!

"But I enjoy your spunkiness." She continued as she casually inspected her fingernails. I used her disinterest to my advantage and worked harder at my bindings; a loop slipped. "You could do well and be useful to me here in the ranks of The Appointed."

More rope gave. All I needed to do now was shrug off the rest of it; I stopped moving so she wouldn't pick up on the fact that I had come close to regaining my freedom.

I almost laughed. "Join you? I would never join you."

Majie rolled her eyes. "Do you know how many times I've heard that? If I really wanted you to do something, all I would have to do is hold eye contact long enough." She gave me a pointed glare.

I quickly concentrated on the tip of her nose instead of her piercing raven eyes. "So, The Appointed are all held against their will? That's good to know; it should make taking you down easier."

"Very few people aren't here of their own volition." She boasted.

"Somehow, I don't believe you. Seems like a pretty convenient power to have over people and not abuse."

Her brows furrowed. "What would be the fun in that?" Her face smoothed. "If you don't start behaving, I'll have to wake André to deal with you." She gestured toward the coffin in the alcove. "I can assure you; he won't be in the best of spirits being woken up this early."

"Do it." I dared, stopping myself from reaching up and holding my neck; revealing that I had freed myself. I couldn't let her see my fear, so I shoved it deep down and called on the spirit of the fighter.

◆ ◆ ◆

Amusement flickered in her eyes. "You're weak." She feigned concern. "And André detests being woken up at his unnatural hour." She paused thoughtfully. "Let us have some fun and see how the Alpha line is holding up, shall we? Oh, Nickoli." She summoned.

Soon after, I heard another pair of footsteps work their way toward the room. A young man, who appeared to be around nineteen, walked in. I hadn't even considered the possibility she would call for reinforcements.

His moss-green eyes stared vacantly as if he saw nothing around him and he moved in a very mapped-out manner. Coppery red hair swept unkempt around his square face. He wore his chest bare with loose tan pants cinched at the waist held by a plain tan belt. Whatever purpose he served, he looked prepared. Several pockets decorated his pants, with four on the front in a traditional placement and two more situated just above each knee. The lower-left pocket contained something lumpy, but I couldn't make it out. A black choker with a gleaming jade pendant sat a little too snugly under his Adam's apple. He sported a lean physique and looked like he could pose a decent challenge in hand-to-hand combat.

Majie glided across the room to the couch, and he followed. "Attack." She said nonchalantly as she took a seat.

Every muscle in Nickoli's body tensed with that one word, and he sprang.

I released my hands and shoved myself into a standing position just in time to avoid him crushing into me.

Something seemed animalistic about him, but he wasn't a wolf like me.

He shot to his feet and slashed a hand in my direction. Suddenly, his fingers weren't fingers anymore. The first knuckle joint of each finger had transformed into a pointed claw. I had to force myself back down to the ground to avoid the attack.

A shapeshifter.

When I righted myself, I felt dizzy; Majie was right about one thing; I was weak. If I couldn't get out of here soon, he would defeat me. I squirmed between him and the couch to prevent getting pinned against the wall.

Majie had left the door unguarded; all I needed to do was get to it.

He came at me again. I dodged by rolling in the door's direction.

Throughout all the fighting, his eyes remained vacant. He looked fierce yet placid at the same time.

I sprang back to avoid his kick. Another foot closer to the door.

The pendant at his neck pulsed before each move he made. Could it be some sort of holding curse? Majie said they held some members against their will; maybe if I could get the choker off, he could help me escape.

I dared not look at Majie to see if she saw through my plan; a glance could give it all away if she hadn't.

This time when he attacked, I stepped toward him instead of away. I grabbed the choker with both hands and kicked his torso as I yanked.

The choker broke, and he stumbled backward. I wanted to howl with victory, but it would have been short-lived if I did. He launched into me and tackled me to the floor.

Bewildered, I put my hands up to defend my face. His eyes no longer looked vacant. They seemed scared.

He landed a hard punch on my left side.

"Run!" I wheezed. My vision went blurry, and the light in the room started to sparkle. I hadn't hit my head, but I didn't have the time to figure out what was happening.

His arm reared back for another punch. "Run!" I barked at him.

In an instant, he flew off of me and toward the door. I crawled a foot before getting back up to my feet in my attempt to follow him.

Beside the door sat a pack that looked suspiciously like the one I brought from home. I grabbed it as I ran through the doorway and slung it onto my shoulders.

Majie's outraged screams followed us. Nickoli seemed to know where he was going, so I followed his lead.

The door flung open to reveal a shady, covered pathway connecting several doors together, and zigzagging, presumably, leading to more doors out of sight. Nickoli bolted to the right, ignoring the designated walkways. As soon I noticed an opening, I dug deep, put on a burst of speed, and surpassed Nickoli. I ran for the cover of the woods, and Nickoli followed suit.

CHAPTER 9

Waves of dread washed over me as we ran. I shouldn't be running. Alphas never run; they stay and fight. Uncle taught me that since youth. If one dreams of becoming Alpha, as I do, they have to be the strongest, and the strong don't turn tail and run from any enemy. Alphas are leaders because they are the best.

I can't let myself go back to the pack now. They couldn't know I ran. I can't bear seeing the look of disappointment on Uncle's face.

Any dreams I had of obtaining clout in the pack were now squashed. Nothing would redeem me from this shame.

Someone running at me from the tree line interrupted my downward spiral into a depressed thought process. I lunged, grabbed whoever it was by the back of the head, and introduced their face to my knee. The body went limp, and a small trickle of blood ran down my leg from their nose. I littered them on the ground like a piece of garbage, not too far from reality for an Appointed member. It felt good to at least do some damage as we retreated, but it didn't negate the shame of retreating.

As soon as we crossed the threshold of trees, vines shot out around us, wrapping around our ankles and aiming for our wrists.

"Majie's magic! Trying to slow us down!" Yelled Nickoli. Despite the chaos swirling around us, I couldn't help but notice his voice laced with a prominent, but not overpowering, Russian accent. His tone sat in the lower range and had a sense of dignity to it.

Turning my attention back to our situation, I noted the vines appeared to only come from one direction.

I kicked away the vines around my ankles and shrug off the ones trying to restrain my hands. "Follow!" I barked and took off, running along the tree line.

He followed without hesitation.

He would make an excellent pack member; clipped sentences and a crude understanding are all excellent traits a pack needs to accomplish a mission.

The vines couldn't keep up with us, and after running three yards, I spotted an opening and charged through with Nickoli right behind me.

Twigs and low branches scratched my skin and pulled at my hair. From the corner of my eye, I could see thin red lines appearing on Nickoli's exposed skin.

By now, Nickoli took the lead. He jumped, and his body shimmered. Where Nickoli had just been, a handsome, red falcon now flew.

Many thanks to the witch who invented enchanted clothing, so shapeshifters and werewolves no longer had to strip naked before transforming. It would make for some incredibly awkward situations, let alone with someone you just met.

I sped up to match his speed and kept my eyes locked on his bird form as trees whizzed by in a blur.

I don't know how long we ran before my legs began to sing out in protest. Despite pumping my legs harder and harder, I still fell behind and eventually had to stop.

The bird shimmered, and Nicholi stood before me. His chest moved up and down rapidly as he tried to catch his breath, but he still held his composure while I heaved unattractively for breath.

He stared at me, and after a few seconds, he spoke. "You're a werewolf?"

I nodded and flopped down on the ground. I took off the backpack and peeked inside; yup, this was mine!

I couldn't help but giggle at my luck while rummaging through it for a canteen. The contents sloshed inside as I retrieved it. I took the cap off and sniffed it—water, delicious, plain water.

"Water?" I offered him and laughed a little. Exhaustion started to set in, making me a little delirious.

Skeptically he took it, and I fished another canteen out for myself. I gulped down about half the container, which was more than I should have, but I couldn't help it. In that moment, water tasted like a divine gift.

"Want some food?" I asked after I composed my manic giggling. He shook his head and cautiously sat opposite to me.

I shrugged, pulled out two sticks of dried venison, tore off a sizeable chunk of bread, and devoured them. My stomach begged for more, but I dared not satisfy it fully. Who knows when I'll be able to replenish my supplies?

After I had just put on my backpack back, we heard leaves rustling in the distance. Nickoli shot up, and I clamored to my feet to look around.

"Can you run?" He asked.

"Doesn't seem like I have a choice."

"Follow me; I saw a place we can hide in."

He shimmered back into a falcon as soon as I nodded.

I settled back into a steady run speed, but the woods fought back with branches pulling at my hair and scratching my skin, and roots trying to jump up and catch my feet. I had to force my legs to keep pace.

No torture could compare to how it felt running in that moment. I kept trying to slow down, but as soon as I did, Nickoli would circle back and peck me - not hard enough to break skin but a painful pinch nonetheless - to keep me going before retaking the lead.

We came upon a mountain, and Nickoli forced me to climb. Roughly twenty-five feet up, I barely made it to a ledge. Shakily, I pulled myself up and noticed a small cave opening big enough to fit no more than four grown adults.

I took one step forward toward the mouth of the cave before my legs gave out. My eyes rolled to the back of my head, and my world gave way to darkness for the second time.

CHAPTER 10

Nickoli

She reached the top of the ledge, but just barely. At least she made it. I turned my attention toward securing our temporary hideout, but scraping noises stole my focus back to her. She looked incredibly weak, and her feet dragged against the stone as she lost the ability to take full steps forward. She started to sink. Luckily, I caught her just as her knees gave out underneath her. As soon as our skin connected, I gasped in surprise and let go of her. Gravity took control once again, and she sank to the ground. My hands shot out to cushion her head.

I quickly let go once she was out of danger of cracking her head open.

Who is this girl, and what was that? Some sort of after-effect of Majie's control?
My ears picked up on something moving in the woods below us.

My brows furrowed as I thought of our next move. I needed to get her inside, but I hesitated at the idea of touching her again. I looked at her unconscious form; it did not look like she would be waking up on her own anytime soon.

I set my jaw in determination, knowing my best option would be to pick her up. I slipped one arm under her neck and one arm under her knees. As I lifted, the shimmer took over. Colors appeared brighter, and everything looked like when sunlight hits water.

I glanced at her slack face in awe; I had never seen someone more beautiful. Her nose had a slight crook in it from getting broken at least once, but probably more than that, since she seemed to know how to handle herself. I should have been in more of a hurry to get into the cave, but at that moment, I had never felt so content. Her sand-colored hair swung free as I walked us inside. I had to stifle a giggle as her hair tickled my arm.

As soon as I set her down, dull reality set back in hard and abruptly. I caught myself craving the sensation again, but couldn't give in. We weren't in the clear just yet. I needed to get some work done. *"What's wrong with me?"* I thought. *I don't know this girl.* The only logical conclusion was that this had to be a side-effect of being imprisoned by that witch. It had to be.

I shimmied the backpack out from under her, impressing myself by doing it without touching her again, and unclipped the sleeping roll from the top. After I rolled it out, my jaw tightened as I looked at her unconscious form. Unfortunately, there was no way to avoid touching her during this next part. I lined everything up and squeezed my eyes shut. As if dared to plunge my hands into ice water, grabbing her under the arms, and yanking her onto the laid-out mat. I opened my eyes and shrugged. Good enough. She now laid mostly on the mat. I needed to secure our location, so I wasn't too concerned with placing her perfectly.

 As I turned to busy myself with the next task, something soft caught my eye, and I noticed the corner of a small pillow sticking out of her bag. Even though I tried placing it under her head fast, the color effect still happened. I made a mental note to just avoid touching her until I could figure out what was going on.

I got up to leave but thought to myself that she must have packed a blanket if she had packed a pillow. After some quick rummaging, I proved myself correct. I whipped out the small brown throw blanket and tucked it around her.

Satisfied with my work, I jumped up and transformed into a falcon. I flew out of the cave and gathered as many sticks as I could carry.

Once back, I started a small fire and got to work.

CHAPTER 11

Leza

I woke up on a mat, a pillow under my head, and a blanket tucked around me. I took a deep breath in and smiled as I smelled home, but when I opened my eyes, I wasn't home. Rather, cold stone surrounded me—the cave; I remembered. Before emerging from sleep completely, I could almost forget about my new shame and future riddled with guilt if I returned to the pack. I groaned and rolled over. A small fire emanated a comfortable warmth several feet away from me and illuminated my immediate surroundings. Nickoli must have gone through my things! I spied a canteen, and some food laid out within arm's reach. Nickoli definitely went through my things. I scowled. Sitting up took tremendous effort; my bones felt as heavy as the surrounding rocks.

As I looked around, I sipped at the canteen and nibbled on the food. My stomach ordered me to eat faster, but my throat didn't want to swallow.

◆　◆　◆

I could spot a defined turn behind the fire, making this more of a tunnel than a cave, and I was alone.

I turned to where the entrance to the cave should have been, but only saw a solid rock face. The sound of approaching footsteps interrupted my confusion, and a shadow moved just before my line of sight of the turn. Without thinking, and with food still in my mouth, I tried to growl. What should have been a low intimidating rumble from my chest came out as dry, choking coughs as a piece of bread lodged itself down the wrong pipe.

A rich laugh echoed from the tunnel as I cleared my throat with some water from the canteen.

"Scary." Nickoli teased, and I scowled at him, embarrassed.

He seemed to sit as far away from me as possible. He wasn't quite staring at me, but he wasn't really looking away from me, either.

The fire crackled, but it wasn't enough to drown out the awkwardness I felt because of his not-quite-staring.

"This cave didn't seem to be this big from the outside," I announced.

"It wasn't."

I raised an eyebrow. "You're just a shapeshifter; how did you move rock? And how did you plug the entrance?" He reached into one of his pockets and pulled out a vial. I got up from my mat and sat closer to get a better look. As I approached, he flinched slightly, and he looked as if he had momentarily wanted to pull away from me. It had been a while since I last had a bath;

maybe I smelled too bad. Trying not to get any more offended or embarrassed, I shuffled back away from him.

The vial contained a black liquid, but it pulsed with different hues of blues, purples, and greens as the firelight danced across it, like a blackbird in the sun.

"It can cut through anything or reseal it if you have the same material. I've used it to cut through the mountain as a shortcut to the other side."

"That's very handy."

"Yeah, I always think I'm going to stump him when I think of crazy potions, but he always comes back with a working product. Exactly what I ask for."

"Can I try it?" He hesitated, but tossed the vial to me. I went over to the nearest wall and uncorked it. I didn't expect the tiny brush attached to the inside of the cork.

"Now, draw a circle using a clockwise motion," he instructed. As soon as I did so, the rock in front of me glowed red hot. "Get ready to catch it!" I barely stuck my hand out in time before I caught the piece in my hands. I produced a sigh of relief when I discovered the glow was simply cosmetic, and not an indicator of temperature. "Now, hold it to where it fell and draw the circle counter-clockwise." This time, the rock glowed, but it stayed in place. I ran my hand across it; it felt smooth and undisturbed. I squinted at it, but couldn't find any marks indicating anything had ever happened.

"Amazing," I said as I handed the vial back to him and returned to sit on my mat. "I'd like to have a friend like that."

Another silence followed. I fidgeted with a string attached to my mat.

"How did The Appointed capture you?" I asked quietly. When I looked up, Nickoli's expression had darkened, and he avoided eye contact

He finally answered, just as I thought he intended to ignore the question. "My community has a place in these mountains where we meet for supplies." He gestured vaguely around us.

"Some friends and I were on our way to pick up a shipment when The Appointed ambushed us."

Mountains, as in plural, meant a chain, and if he's a shapeshifter, that could only mean one thing. "Wait, are we in the Connecting Mountains? The one that connects the shapeshifter and witch territories?" Nickoli nodded. I was a very, very, very long way from home. I felt they would never welcome me back with my shame, but despite that, the notion of how far I'd gone made me anxious. "But no one lives on the other side of the Connecting Mountains except for shipwrecked humans. Just like it is with the Border Mountains in the south."

"That's what I'd been told too. Looks like that's some trick Majie pulled off because it's definitely the hiding place of The Appointed."

I furrowed my brow. At least I know now. Maybe I can get a message to my pack through a traveling peddler.

"Majie relies on her followers to do her bidding, but she's still very dangerous. She underestimated you, and you caught her off guard; that's the only reason we escaped."

"How long was I there?"

"Almost a day."

I sat and chewed over that answer. I didn't like it. A journey on foot in the Connecting Mountains would have been too long to keep me alive and unconscious, but a vampire can travel great distances when it taps into its full speed, or he could have used a portal.

I reached over to continue eating the food laid out for me. Between bites, I asked, "Can you tell me more?"

Nickoli shook his head. "I don't know much more. We weren't there when André brought you in. Majie kept me with her at all times. I tried to escape too many times, so Majie trapped me in my own body. She-"

"How long were you there?" I blurted out.

His brows pulled together as he thought. "I think a month, maybe a little more."

"You don't know?"

"It's not like I could make notches on the wall to keep track of the days."

I didn't want to make him angry. "What happened to your friends?"

"We fought and ran. I never saw them at The Appointed's camp, so I don't know what happened to them." The subject clearly agitated him.

"I'm sorry."

After a moment, Nickoli picked back up where he left off before my interruption. "Majie didn't like that he brought you back. She demanded to know everything about you. Once she learned you were of "The Alpha Line", she grew angrier with him. What does that mean, by the way? Being from The Alpha Line."

"Our leader is called the Alpha, and a fight to the death decides the next Alpha. Well, it doesn't have to actually be to the death. If you tapped out, then you lose, but werewolves can be stubborn." I smirked a little. "The Alpha has come from my family line since our ancestors first came to the island. The current Alpha is my uncle."

Nickoli raised his eyebrows and seemed impressed. "Anyway, once she learned that, she wanted to handle things herself. André doing things on his own really miffed her."

"What is their relationship? Majie and André's?"

"I'm not sure. They're close. Or they used to be close, but it feels like they're drifting apart. Maybe they are, or were, at one point lovers? They spend a lot of time together, but snip and gripe at each other often."

◆ ◆ ◆

I opened my mouth to ask another question, but muffled noises cut me off and grabbed our attention. It sounded close. "What was that?" I whispered, alarmed.

"Pack up." He ordered, and I obeyed, quickly shoving everything back into my backpack. "Place a hand on the wall and follow me."

CHAPTER 12

André

André's eyebrows furrowed in annoyance as he awoke to some commotion outside of his coffin. "I just want to sleep." He grumbled aloud in complaint.

Still under the light influence of sleep, his mind felt foggy, and he had a hard time processing what he was hearing.

Waking a vampire after sunrise is incredibly difficult, but the "dream" Majie had tortured him with had already put André on edge.

Anger flooded his mind as he realized he would not be going back to sleep. He could make out the sounds now, sounds of flesh pounding flesh, the sound of a fistfight. Only an hour had passed since sunrise.

He reached out to open the lid of his coffin as someone started screeching. It sounded like nails on a chalkboard.

He sprang from his resting place to see Majie pointing at the open door.

"Go after them!" She demanded.

He gave her an incredulous look. "I can't go after them; it's full daylight!"

Majie choked out a sound of frustration. She reached for anything close to her and threw them in a rage. A pillow from the couch bounced off the wall. That wasn't satisfying enough, so she flipped the coffee table over, tipping a bottle that landed at her feet.

"Majie, stop!" André barks. "These are my things!"

Majie grabbed the bottle by the neck and hurled it. André tracked it with his eyes as it found its mark too close to the oil painting of Maria. It shattered upon impact, and wine seeped its way into the canvas. André's whole body became still and ridged.

"Don't be so dramatic; it's easy to clean up."

André didn't care. Even as Majie waved her hand without a care, and the stain faded, he turned toward her and went berserk.

He closed the short distance between them in less than half a heartbeat. His mouth foamed as he snarled. One hand went for her throat. One of his long-pointed fingernails had grazed her cheek, but he couldn't move.

The fury that blazed in Majie's eyes was unfathomable.

"You dare turn your stinking hands on me?" Her voice boomed deep and loud as thunder. She rose, and André lifted into the air.

Her voice returned to normal. "I think you need to go back to sleep." She flung him. The wall cracked when he made contact. "I highly suggest you think about your actions." She walked to the door, paused, then quietly concluded, "Do that again, and next time I will throw you out into the daylight and relish in your screams." She left, and the spell over André broke.

CHAPTER 13

Leza

Total darkness swallowed us only after a few paces. Curiously, I held my hand up to my nose, but could not see it.

"I would have expected them to reach the mountain sooner." Nickoli's disembodied voice said from somewhere in front of me.

"How long have we been here?" I echoed.

"Sun has to be rising now."

I had to break this new habit of blacking out and waking up hours later.

The tunnel never stayed straight for long. I felt like we were zigzagging straight through the middle of the rock.

"Where are we going?"

"Somewhere safe," he replied.

After a few more turns, I could make out the silhouette of Nickoli and a very faint light up ahead. I wasn't paying attention when I exited the tunnel and tripped over a large, round rock, falling straight into Nickoli. As soon as our skin touched, the world became brighter, which I initially thought odd for an overcast morning. A moment before, the world had appeared appropriately hazy. Indistinct objects suddenly looked crisp and well-defined. I found my footing again and stepped back away from him. The world returned to its normal hue. I shook my head, making sure the colors wouldn't just change again.

Nickoli stood stiff as a board. He didn't turn around but asked, "Are you alright?"

"Fine. Light change must have messed me up, I guess." I blinked several more times and gave a nervous laugh. "Yeah, I'm okay now."

Still without turning, he said, "We don't have much further to go," and continued walking.

I followed him, keeping an extra close eye on the terrain so I wouldn't experience another misstep.

◆ ◆ ◆

Several hours passed, and the sun glared in the sky. Nickoli's skin adopted a sheen of sweat. Freckles trailed from one to the other across his wide shoulders, like his own mountain chain right there on his body. I suppressed the urge to reach out and trace it with my fingers. *In no culture, would it be okay to just start stroking a stranger. What's wrong with me?*

The mountainous terrain sloped, and the slope gave way to a forest, and the forest gave way to a village.

The buildings looked like exact duplicates of each other, but some contained more stories than others, and they all wore different colors of paint. They stood spaced evenly apart, with each having its own decently sized yard. Children's toys littered some yards, some had a garden or two, and some even had a table and chairs set up for gatherings. I could tell these buildings housed the local people, but they looked very different from the huts back home. These homes were constructed from wood, like the council building, whereas our homes typically consist of a combination of mud and straw.

Nickoli led me between two of the buildings, and we came onto a street. He picked up the pace as he followed the road. After several yards, he entered a full-on run, and I had trouble keeping up with him. We raced past people in their yards. Some shouted after us, but Nickoli didn't stop.

We headed straight for a three-story building. The bottom section was rectangular, making it longer than the upper square-shaped sections. Figures moved by a large window and I slowed my pace. Nickoli barreled over small oval stones that created the pathway, which led to three small steps before the door. I thought he was going to plow right through it, but he froze. The people inside must have seen us and thrown the door open in response. In the now-open doorway stood the biggest man I had ever seen. He was tall and burly, with a beard that masked the bottom half of his face. His hair matched Nickoli, and they shared the same nose.

They just stared at each other. The man's eyes widened in bewilderment.

"Papa?" Nickoli's voice caught in his throat.

The man's dark blue eyes twinkled as he wrapped his arms around his son, engulfing him in a giant bear hug.

I felt as if I was invading a private moment, so turned my focus back to the details of the house.

Two great windows flanked the door. The second story had two evenly spaced smaller windows, and one more window sat centered on the third story. Dark beige paint and a cobalt trim colored the house. The structure itself emitted warmth and love.

"Edik, who's at the door?" A woman asked as she came into view. Her eyes were the exact same color as Nickoli's. The man stepped aside for her to see, and she let out a cry. She rushed to Nickoli, grabbed his face, and smothered his cheeks and forehead in kisses. She murmured something in a language that I couldn't understand.

"Mama," Nickoli said. Tears ran freely down their faces.

His mother led him out of view, and his father motioned me closer.

"What is your name?" His accent laced his words a lot thicker than Nickoli's, but his tone sounded jovial.

"Leza, sir." Unsure of their customs, I bowed respectfully.

"You saved our son?"

"Well...we took turns."

He nodded and clasped an enormous hand around my shoulder, ushering me into his home and closing the door behind us. We stood in a short hallway with an opening on either side of us. He crossed to the right, where Nickoli and his mother sat chatting on a couch.

Footsteps sounded from the story above. A petite girl, no more than fourteen, came bounding down the stairs. She smoothed down her shirt. "Mama, where is-" She stopped mid-sentence when she noticed Nickoli. "Nickoli!" She exclaimed and flew to her family.

They spoke in a strange language, so I had no way of following the conversation. They looked completely absorbed in one another, so I stood unnoticed in the doorway, watching. Both the mother and the girl had strawberry blonde hair and freckled like Nickoli.

The father was not what I would have expected of a man that size. Someone as big as him back home would have been stoic, always putting on airs to be intimidating, but this man appeared warm and spoke animatedly.

Nickoli looked so relaxed. He smiled ear to ear, and tears still fell down his cheeks. He was mesmerizing at that moment. A boy, happy to be home.

As I looked over each family member, the mother made eye contact with me. I quickly averted my eyes and pretended to examine a piece of art on the wall. I flushed. It was too late; She caught me. I looked back over, and she made a gesture toward me while asking Nickoli something. In his reply, I heard my name. She crossed the room to me and placed a hand on my shoulders. "You brought my son back to us. Thank you!" She pulled me in for a hug, and I awkwardly hugged her back. She released me with a squeeze of my shoulders. "Anna, take Leza up to the guest room. I'm going to fix up some food!" She smiled as she left the room.

◆ ◆ ◆

Anna hugged her brother before getting up from the couch. She walked toward the stairs and stopped at the first step. "Come on, follow me. It's just up here." She smiled politely as she waited.

The second level only had two rooms, with both doors side by side. The only other feature was the next set of stairs.

Anna opened the door closest to us. They had decorated the room with off-white and neutral colors. The room simply contained a bed, a dresser, and a door on either side of the dresser.

She raised her hand toward the wall close to us. I heard a flicking sound before a light came on. I involuntarily flinched.

"What's the matter? You haven't seen a light before?" She giggled.

"No. We don't have any of this."

"Oh." She paused. "What do you use then?"

"Fire, potions, resources around us. What powers this?" I pointed to the source.

"The light? Electricity. Humans have used it on the mainlands for ages. Shapeshifters enlisted the help of witches to make it available here. We built this community after how humans live now. It's very comfortable." She talked very matter-of-fact, and I detected no condescension in her tone, but this conversation made me uncomfortable.

She stayed quiet for a moment, then continued showing around the room. "The closet," she pointed to the door on the far side of the dresser, "and the dresser is for your things." She opened up the other door. "And this is the bathroom." A smooth porcelain bowl attached to the wall greeted us as she opened the door. A basin sat atop a cabinet with a faucet flanked by two nobs, and a big tub sat up against the wall with a physical privacy curtain.

"Indoor plumbing?" She asked. I shook my head no. "You guys must really rough it." She teased.

I got defensive. "We use the land."

"I don't mean to offend. I've never met someone who doesn't have modern conveniences. It's interesting. So, do you know what a toilet is?"

"We have outhouses."

"Same concept, just in the house. You do your business in it, then flush." She pushed down on a silver handle to the side of it to demonstrate. "This is the sink. Left knob is cold," she twisted it on and off. Water flowed from the faucet and into the basin. "Right is for hot." She pulled back the curtain to the tub. "Same for the tub, but pull this up," she lifted a little silver knob on the faucet, "to make the water come out of the shower head. Got it?" I nodded. "Excellent!" She opened up the cabinet under the sink. "Towels, washcloths, and an extra roll of toilet paper."

"Thanks." And with that, Anna left the room, shutting the door behind her.

I stood there, a bit overwhelmed for a moment. I caught my reflection in the bathroom mirror and wished I hadn't. At the moment, I looked pale, grimy, and overall horrendous. No small wonder Anna made the assumptions she did. Looking the way I do, not having the modern conveniences she has, she must think me primitive. I decided a shower was in order. I fished out my soap and potions and noticed a small grouping of bottles on the corner edge of the tub. Labels identified the bottles as soap, shampoo, and conditioner.

I missed the pools back home.

CHAPTER 14

Nickoli

I feared this was all just a dream. That, at any second, Majie would snap her fingers, and I would find myself back in her clutches. The skin around my neck itched. Majie kept the collar too tight to add to my discomfort.

Now that I regained my freedom and control of my own body, I had to stop myself from jerking around just because I could. To move when I wanted to move was something that I would never take for granted again.

The old couch never felt so comfortable. The slight sag in its cushions almost felt like a warm embrace, as if even the furniture welcomed me home with glee. Nothing had ever felt so good, nothing except for when I touched her. At the thought of her, my eyes snapped up in time to watch her disappear up the stairs.

Was she looking back at me? My cheeks flushed, and I knew Papa was looking at me.

I cleared my throat, awkwardly. "What happened to the rest of the guys? I never saw them–" fear prevented me from invoking that place's name, "-where I was." I finished.

Papa's face darkened. "We looked everywhere for you boys. Like you, we never found Ezra." My heart raced, but he continued before I could respond. "They didn't take Sawyer, though!"

I perked up. "Sawyer is safe?"

"Yes, son. They beat him badly, but somehow he got away."

"It was a blitz attack. I think they were after our airdrop supplies."

Papa nodded. "A good portion of that was gone as well." His eyes met mine, full of emotion, begging for my understanding. "We looked everywhere for you. They must have used magic, portals, or both because we never figured out which way they went or where they came from."

"Papa, it's okay." I patted one of his gigantic hands in reassurance. "We were never prepared for something like this. Don't beat yourself up over it."

With his other hand, Papa wiped at his teary eyes. "The mayor will have to hear about this. Half the town contented themselves to write this off as a freak accident." Papa's voice rose slightly in anger.

"нет. This wasn't an accident. Those people have been stirring up more and more trouble. Our town is going to have to learn to defend itself."

Papa engulfed me in another hug. " I'm so sorry, Сын."

CHAPTER 15

Leza

By the time I cleaned up, food scents wafted up the stairs to greet my nostrils. My mouth salivated when I detected meat. My stomach rumbled, and I quickly toweled off my hair before brushing it. I donned a white tank top and some khaki shorts and left my hair hanging damp to air dry. Before joining my hosts downstairs, I walked to the mirror, hoping I looked more presentable now. I did, but my skin still looked pale, and my eyes locked onto the two pink circles on my neck. I frowned, then situated my hair to cover it.

The scent of bread, potatoes, chicken, cabbage, and cheese caught my attention in full force; my stomach grumbled so loud I knew it was time to follow them.

My nose led me down the steps, around the corner, through the dining room, and into the room with tantalizing scents.

Nickoli's mother pulled a pan from a hot metal contraption. Back home, we either cooked over a fire or, truthfully, some day's meat just tasted better raw. Curiously, I didn't see any potatoes, chicken, cabbage, or cheese, the pan only contained what looked like individual bread loaves.

She used tongs to arrange the loaves onto a large serving plate as she greeted me. "How do you like the guest room, Leza? Is it all right? Is everything you need in there?"

"Yes, ma'am. It's like nothing I've ever seen before." She gave me a warm, comforting smile. "Is there anything I can help you with?"

She tsked at me. "Don't be silly! You're our guest; you don't have to do anything." She exited the kitchen and set the plate on the table in the dining room. Someone had pulled a mismatched chair up to the table. Clearly, the table typically sat only four people. She called something out, again in that language I didn't understand, and gave me another one of her warm smiles as she took a seat. The rest of the family leaked into the dining room and took their respective seats. The mother and father sat side by side, and opposite them sat Nickoli and Anna. They had squeezed my mismatched chair in between the kids.

The father reached over and placed a loaf on his plate, and everyone else followed suit. Gingerly, I picked one up and put it on my plate. The bread felt soft, but it had something inside of it.

I mimicked Nickoli by cutting into the loaf with a fork and knife. Seductive food smells and steam rose, and I had to control myself from abandoning my utensils and diving face-first into my plate.

I stabbed a hefty bite onto my fork and plunged it into my mouth, immediately regretting that I didn't blow on it first. My face contorted in response to the sudden pain, and I tried quietly exhaling some of the heat and take a sip of water to cool down my now-burning mouth. Anna stifled a giggle.

Other than that, the room remained silent, save for forks and knives clinking against plates. I couldn't help but feel like the silence was my fault. I keep my eyes trained down on my plate. Out of the corner of my eye, I saw Nickoli take another loaf, so I did the same.

The silence gnawed at me. I looked up from my plate to address his mother. "This food is delicious, ma'am. What is it? There's definitely nothing like this back home."

"Pirozhki." She replied, and I nodded like I knew what that meant. "Where are you from?" She asked.

"We live at the bottom of Velcom Mountain. It's south of here."

"Just your family?" Anna asked.

I looked at her, a little confused. "The entire pack does." And then the silence began again.

Anna got up and took her dishes to the sink. I gathered up my dishes and copied Anna, making a conscious effort to avoid going in for thirds.

Once I left the room, I heard the family start quietly talking, though I couldn't understand any of it. They quieted down when I appeared in the doorway again.

Anna now stood beside her mother. "Will you come with me?" She asked.

I felt the whole family staring at me. "Um, sure."

"Excellent!" She beamed and crossed the room. She linked her arm with mine and almost pulled me out of the room.

Anna stopped at the front door and slipped some shoes on. She looked down at my bare feet. "Where're your shoes? Do you need to go up and get them?"

"I don't wear shoes."

"You don't wear shoes? That must make getting ready so convenient!" She laughed and ushered me down the street.

◆ ◆ ◆

I let her lead me to a small square lined with a variety of shops. The setup reminded me of the peddlers that occasionally visit the pack. The difference here is that these shops were permanent, while the peddlers used temporary tents or vardos to display their wares. We walked straight toward a storefront that displayed dresses and outfits in its window.

"What are we doing?" I asked her as we neared the door.

"I'm getting you some presents. A thank you from the family for bringing Nickoli back."

I halted, forcing her to an abrupt stop. "No. You don't -"

She cut me off. "No use protesting. It will offend Mama if you're not properly thanked."

I groaned in defeat and let her drag me into the shop. They graciously invited me into their home; I didn't want to offend anyone.

A bell tinkled as we entered. The shop contained racks of girly dresses, clothes, and accessories everywhere.

"Mrs. Gretta?" Anna called, and a small woman in her seventies descended a set of stairs behind the counter.

"Anna? Is that you, dear?" She fumbled with some bifocals that hung from her neck. "Anna! It is you! How's your mother doing? I've been so worried about you all. I've just been beside myself. Awful thing that happened." She took notice of me. "Who's your friend, dear? Are you new to the Island? I've never seen you around before."

"This is Leza," Anna answered for me. "She brought Nickoli back."

Mrs. Gretta clasped her hands together. "Thank the heavens. Nickoli is back! Tell your mother I'll be over for a visit once I close up the shop."

Anna nodded. "I brought Leza here for a treat as a thank you."

Mrs. Gretta shook her head in agreement. "Yes, yes. Pick anything you like, dear. It's on the house!"

I didn't have time to thank the old woman before Anna whirled me around to a rack of sundresses.

"Mrs. Gretta used to babysit Nickoli and me when we were younger to help Mama out." Anna babbled on while she thumbed through the dresses, leaving me in a semi-daze as I contemplated how I got into this situation.

I never wore dresses. They're not practical to fight in. They either have too much fabric that can get caught on something, or they're too tight and restrict your range of motion.

Aimlessly, I followed Anna around while she commented on this or that. I did my best to utter "mmha" and other noises of agreement when appropriate. She abruptly stopped in front of a mannequin, which caught me off-guard and I bumped into her.

"Perfect!" she exclaimed, ignoring the incident. She whipped the dress off the mannequin with such an impressive speed it didn't even wobble and tossed the dress my way.

I held the dress out to get a better look at it. It was strapless and short; it would fall at least mid-thigh on me. The top of the dress was dark blue and washed out to a blue, so light it almost appeared white.

"Do you see those red curtains?" She asked. I surveyed the room, then nodded once I spotted them to the left of a wall of accessories- handbags, shoes, jewelry. "That's where you change. I'm going to see if there is anything else over here, then I'll be right over." Anna abruptly turned to hunt through the other racks. She reminded me of a cat stalking a mouse.

Mrs. Gretta stood over by the dressing rooms and held a curtain back for me. "Let me know if there is anything I can help you with, dear." I smiled at her, and she let the curtain fall back into place. I undressed and kicked my clothes into the corner, then slid the dress on. The back wall had a full-length mirror. I straightened my posture and turned to see how I looked. The top of the dress clung under my armpits, and the bottom had a subtle pleat, making it flare just a little. The dark blue complimented my complexion. My face lit up in approval, surprised by how nicely it fit. I frowned at my hair, which had already started frizzing. I ran my fingers through it, attempting to brush it down, and absentmindedly swayed side to side, making the bottom of the dress sway with a dainty *swish* in response to the motion.

"Leza?" Anna called. "Are you ready?"

I stood in the dressing room a moment longer before pulling back the curtain and striding out. Dresses were out of my element, but I didn't want to disappoint her.

Anna leaned over the counter, whispering to Mrs. Gretta, but stopped as soon as I appeared. Both of their heads turned at the same time.

Anna's eyes let up. "I knew it, perfect!" She walked over and started playing with my hair with a perplexed expression on her face.

Mrs. Gretta reached under the counter and laid out a big handful of little white flowers. She grabbed a small stool and lugged it around the counter.

"You are brilliant, Mrs. Gretta." Anna approved as Mrs. Gretta went to retrieve the flowers.

Anna sat me on the stool and pulled all my hair to my back. She ran her fingers through it and commented, "I'm so jealous of your hair. It has the natural waviness I wish I had." My eyes widened in concern as the pink marks on my neck became exposed, but no one mentioned them. I felt vulnerable.

Mrs. Gretta's fingers replaced Anna's fingers, and she started to French braid my hair. Her fingers worked with a surprising nimbleness for how old she was. Anna took a little flower and skillfully placed it in my hair. Simultaneously, working around, and with, Mrs. Gretta.

"How long until the flowers wilt?" I asked, trying to make small talk.

"They're fake, dear. They won't wilt." Mrs. Gretta answered.

Anna held one out for me, and I turned it a few times between my fingers. The flower felt soft, but not right. I handed it back to Anna, and she continued with her task.

Once they finished, Mrs. Gretta retrieved a hand mirror and led me back to the dressing room to view my new hairdo. She left the back hair hanging loose, and the two braided sides melted perfectly into the loose hair. Anna had expertly placed the flowers into the braids.

Anna came up behind me. "You look so pretty!" I blushed a little and mumbled a thank you. I noticed she held a bag that looked like it contained more clothes. As she gathered up my clothes from the floor, I asked what she was holding.

"Don't worry about it." She answered, stuffing my clothes into the bag. "Just another outfit for you. Ready to go back home?" She didn't wait for my reply before she headed for the door.

"Thank you, Mrs. Gretta," I called as I hurried out after Anna. I had to be mindful of my stride in this dress, or else someone could see more of me than I felt comfortable sharing.

While Anna's bossiness may be a little off-putting at first, I like her the more I spent time around her.

"Thanks for the clothes," I said once I caught up to her.

"Don't mention it. You saved my brother. I'll get you all the clothes you could want." Her response made me smile. My parents never had any more children, so it was heartwarming to see the affection Anna had for Nickoli.

Day transitioned into evening. The sun still had some time in the sky before it dipped under the horizon, so it would still take a while before it cooled down outside. I tilted my head up to feel its warmth on my neck and covered my scars with my hand.

"Were you scared?" Anna quietly asked.

"What?" I dropped my hand down to my side.

"When it got you, were you scared?"

I thought a moment before answering. "I wasn't conscious for most of the time it had me. When I was conscious, all I knew was that I had to get out of there. It wasn't until after we escaped for the fear set it."

"And Nickoli?"

I took a longer pause before answering. "I don't know, but I would assume so. An evil witch had placed Nickoli under a spell when I met him. Truthfully, Nickoli saved me more than I saved him. I only provided him with the means of escape, then he led us here."

"You still helped him, and for that, we are forever thankful," Anna stated confidently.

I liked that Anna still felt grateful, despite hearing how little I did. The family was so nice, and I would hate to disappoint them. I had already let the pack down.

Something had been toying at the back of my mind ever since she gave me the tour of the modern bathroom, so I decided finally to ask. "How do you know how humans live?"

She gave me a quizzical look, surprised by the sudden topic change. "Earlier, when you talked about electricity and stuff, you said the humans have had it for years. How do you know that?"

Mama and Papa moved here only a year before they had Nikoli. "We also visit family back in Russia once a year. Have you only ever been on the island?"

I nodded. "I don't know anyone on the mainlands. My family has always lived here."

Anna linked arms with me again as we walked back to her house.

CHAPTER 16

I took my things from Anna, thanked her again, and headed straight to the room they lent me, shutting the door behind me.

I set the bag of clothes on top of the dresser, then plopped down on the bed, letting out an enormous sigh as my body crashed against the plush surface. The day had been really overwhelming, but couldn't go to bed yet, so I decided I should try to be sociable.

When I opened the door to leave the room, Nickoli was standing there with his fist raised to knock.

"Hi." He said and tried to put his arm down in a non-awkward fashion, but it didn't work. His eyes widened as they drank in my new appearance.

I blushed. "Hi."

"Anna?" He asked.

"Yeah, she sort of took over." Not having anything else to fiddle with, I crossed my arms behind my back and held on to opposite elbows, accentuating my chest. Did I want him to look? I think I did. His eyes flickered down just for a moment before training back on my face.

"It's nice. It highlights your bright blue eyes."

My cheeks flushed some more, and I looked away. "Thanks."

Nickoli wore a fresh pair of shorts and a tee shirt that clung to his torso.

"Your family seems nice. They're thrilled you're back." I said, changing the subject.

"It's good to be home. What about your family? They've got to be missing you."

I hung my head. "I can't go back home after retreating. It's shameful to run from a fight."

He reached out toward me, but stopped himself and put his hand back down by his side. "They wouldn't be glad that you're alive?"

Father definitely would, and probably Mother, but the rest of the pack would alienate me. It wouldn't be the same, so I just replied, "No."

"I'm glad."

"Excuse me?" I looked up at him. His expression was soft, and his eyes were inviting.

"I'm glad you're alive." He replied, and the corner of his lips turned up into a smile.

Slowly, I felt myself leaning in towards him involuntarily, but it felt so natural that I didn't fight or question it. He leaned in too. We moved like two magnets drawn toward one another. I was a fraction away from him. His scent traveled to my nostrils, sweet and consuming. I let out a small sigh. Just before our lips touched, I heard footsteps coming up the stairs. My face burned as we took a step back from one another.

Anna came into view.

"Hello, Anna," Nickoli said, annoyed. Probably a standard sibling greeting.

"Hello." She said with a knowing glint in her eye.

Nickoli turned, muttering something, and ascended the second flight of stairs.

"Did I interpret something?" She feigned innocence.

I shook my head and retreated into my room, locking the door behind me. I heard a muffled, mischievous giggle from the hallway.

I got a distinct feeling that Nickoli and I had been set up. Embarrassed and content never to leave this room again, I flopped down on the bed and curled up on my side.

◆ ◆ ◆

Nickoli's comment about my family kept running through my mind. Suddenly, I longed to be in my own bed, in my own hut, nestled in familiar scents. I wanted to see my mother and father again.

Mingled with the thoughts of my parents, I thought about the marks on my neck. Then I realized something terrible. André knew where my parents lived and what they looked like. I cringed at the thought of André's undead hands being anywhere near my mother. He could sneak up on my pack and slaughter them all before they even knew what happened.

I flung myself at the door and fumbled with the handle. I threw it open and made for the second set of stairs, bounding up them, expecting to find a door, but they ended at a wall. A string dangled above my head. I stepped back and pulled it. A small section of the ceiling came down, and a ladder slid out, stopping perfectly at my feet. Quickly, I climbed.

"Nickoli?" I called at the top. I emerged into a small living room. The first thing to greet me was the backside of a small couch. To my right, there stood an open door, through which I could see the corner of a bed. That is where Nickoli came from. He looked at me skeptically this time, instead of with admiration, like before. "Yes?"

"He knows where they are!"

He gave me a puzzled look.

"André knows where my family is, where the pack is! You said he wanted me so he could annoy Majie. What if he goes home looking for me? What do you think he's going to do when he finds that I'm not there?" I took a breath and answered for him. "Kill my mother, then go after my father. Or what about Uncle? Or my friends?" My tone grew more frantic, and I shook from getting so worked up. "Last time they attacked a pack, we barely fought them off."

Nickoli's expression darkened again. " You've fought them before?"

"I helped defend my home." I snapped. Nickoli raised his hands in surrender, but I plunged on. "An Alpha doesn't sit by while her pack is in danger!" I began to pace. "I can't stay here, but I can't go back. Maybe if I go back and warn them, they could forgive me, or maybe I go back, they don't listen, I become an outcast, and then we all die."

"Leza."

I ignored him. "No one will want to be seen with me."

"Leza."

"I'll never get to be Head Alpha–"
"Leza!"

I halted my rant, but not my pacing.

"They were trailing us in the mountains. If André were to do anything, he would either have to clear it by Majie first or sneak off without her knowing." I stopped pacing and stared at him. "My point is, for the moment, your pack is safe. Besides, even if you went back, what would you do? Fight off The Appointed by yourself?"

"I will if I have to!" I growled.

Nickoli, who had remained calm this whole time, let out a laugh. "You can't fight them all by yourself." I gave him a hard look. "You'll need help."

"Help? Help from who?" My tone came off harsher than I intended. "Sorry."

"Let me introduce you to a friend of mine."
Nickoli motioned me down the ladder and led us to the

backyard. At the edge of their property laid a small rock slab with a pentagram etched into it.

He produced a vial of crystal clear liquid from his pocket and poured three drops into the pentagram. The liquid pooled, then stretched itself along the shape of the etching, and the pentagram started to glow.

"Evander." He said loudly and clearly.

The pentagram glowed brighter, and mist hissed out of the shape. Mist rose from the rock and into the vague form of a man. It reminded me of my privacy curtain when I bathe in the springs until the mist solidified into a man in his early twenties with black, slick-backed hair and hazel eyes. He wore a silk shirt colored with a mix of purple and grey, and he had left the top button casually undone. He wore plain black pants paired with basic black shoes. Nickoli was tall, but this man towered over him.

He smoothed out his shirt and looked up. "Coli!"

"You know I only let Mama call me that," Nickoli said sternly.

Silence followed before the two burst into laughter. Evander slouched down to hug Nickoli, lifting him into the air. "I see you're back alive and well," Evander said as he put Nickoli back down.

"I see you didn't worry too much." Nickoli lightly punched him in the arm.

"I didn't have to; Sage saw that you'd end up all right."

"You still could have put in a little effort."

Evander dramatically placed a hand on his heart and feigned a hurt expression. "You don't think I worry about you, Coli."

Nickoli rolled his eyes. "How is Sage?"

"Fine. Getting married. You all should come."

Before Nickoli could respond, a strawberry-blond cat raced past us and launched itself at Evander. He caught it, and it purred loudly as it rubbed its head under his chin. He laughed. "Hello, Anna." He returned her greeting with chin rubs.

"Anna, we're in the middle of talking," Nickoli said in a true older brother tone.

She folded her ears back and shot him a dirty look. She jumped out of Evander's arms and walked away with her tail twitching.

Evander watched her leave with playful fondness in his eyes as if she, too, were his younger sister. Once she had made it a couple of feet away, he turned to me. "And who is this lovely creature?"

"Leza," I answered, holding myself in a commanding manner that usually kept flirty boys at bay. Boys back home like strong girls but not one that overpowers them.

"Ah, Little Alpha from the Velcome pack." He gave an over-exaggerated bow.

My mouth gaped open in surprise. "How did you know that?"

"Potions are very popular among werewolves. That's where most of my business comes from." He explained as he straightened up. "I had some inquiries about love potions from some Velcome boys, and, being the curious person I am, I naturally had to find out the source of their infatuation." I couldn't control the look of horror that crept onto my face. "Oh, don't worry. I don't make love potions. I'm against them in principle. But everyone knows if you want the best potions, you get them from me." He winked. "But with these looks, no wonder the boys wanted to explore every option." Without warning, he swept my hand into his and brought the back of my hand to meet his lips.

Not ten minutes ago, I would have said that nothing would be more embarrassing than being caught almost kissing a guy by his little sister, but learning that some boys from my pack tried to buy love potions to give me from a man I've only just met while standing next to the boy I think I like bumps this situation to the top of the embarrassment list.

He let go of my hand and turned his attention back to Nickoli, whose eyebrows furrowed slightly, but otherwise, he wore a neutral expression. "Now, what can I do for you, Coli? Looking for a love potion, too?"

"No." Nickoli scowled.

Hearing him say that made my heart drop. I don't even know why that hurt me. Of course not. Of course, he shouldn't. Why do I even care?

Determined not to reveal my confusing emotions, I picked up the conversation for him. "What are your views regarding The Appointed?"

Evander looked surprised I even had to ask. "They took my dear Coli. They're horrible. Anyone who believes otherwise deserves to be poisoned." He stated matter-of-factly.

I couldn't help but grin at his response. "Got any friends that agree with you?"

"Certainly. What are you planning?" His eyes gleamed with mischief.

I told him about André and my need to defend the pack.

"All this for one vampire?" Evander asked once I finished my tale.

"André wouldn't go alone." Nickoli finally chimed in. "The Appointed are bullies. They travel in groups and pick on things they view as lesser."

"Plus," I added. "Taking The Appointed down a peg doesn't sound like a bad idea."

"Well, we won't do much good with just witches, one shapeshifter, and one werewolf. Nickoli, know anyone who will help?" Evander asked.

"A few."

"Looks like we have a nice little rebellion forming."

My spirits crumbled. "How do we know my pack will still be in one piece by the time we can organize our band of misfits and get there?"

Evander laughed. "We can get you to your pack now, silly. You can warn them and then meet us back here. It'll take no more than five minutes." He reassured me. He placed a hand on either side of my shoulders and we switched places.

With a wave of his hand, he produced a small white pill. "Have you ever used a portal before?" I shook my head no. "Then you're going to want to take this." He placed the pill in my palm. I hesitated a second before taking it. With the second wave of his hand, he produced another vial of clear liquid.

"But how will I get back? We don't have a pentagram at home?"

Evander smirked. "Don't worry. Just pour the potion, think of the place you want to go, and then say it out loud. We'll be right here waiting for you." Evander poured the potion, then handed me the vial. "Velcome Mountain." He said with a smile.

CHAPTER 17

My body felt submerged under water, but simultaneously like I was falling from the sky. I squeezed my eyes shut, but curiosity got the better of me, and I glanced down at my body. Oh good, I still had a solid form. I'm not sure if my brain would have been able to handle it if I wasn't. I couldn't make out any details of my surroundings; all I could see was a gray mist.

It didn't take long for the world to come back into focus. I saw a familiar tree line that told me I was home. My feet stood on solid ground again, but as soon as I went to take a step, I retched. I took a moment to compose myself and made sure I hadn't soiled my new dress, before starting my mission to reach Uncle's hut without being spotted. Right now, I didn't want to face anyone. I just wanted to warn Uncle, so I stuck to the tree line as much as possible.

That alone wouldn't be enough to get me there, though. His hut wasn't exactly in the center of the pack, but it felt like it when I wanted to make sure no one saw me.

I watched for a moment before I broke away from the trees. As soon as I did, something big slammed into me, sending me back into the cover of the trees. I hit the ground with a thump, but not hard enough to do any serious damage. I will more than likely have a bump, though.

"Little Alpha?" Deegan had me pinned to the ground. Weirdly, I worried about him messing up my hair. Mrs. Gretta and Anna worked so hard on it. "Where have you been?"

"Get off of me!" I wanted to shout but hissed instead so I wouldn't draw any attention.

Deegan ignored me and took me in. "Nice dress." He commented. "I don't think I've ever seen you in one before."

I squirmed to adjust my dress, as the tackle had risen to a dangerously inappropriate height. "If you don't get off of me, I am going to punch you in the face." I was getting mad.

Deegan didn't budge. You could practically see the word 'lust' written in his eyes. "Little Alpha, this is a once-in-a-lifetime opportunity. Besides, I have the upper hand."

I hid the emotion in my eyes. He started to frighten me, but I couldn't let him see that. "I'll make you a deal. I let you have a kiss, ONE kiss, then you let me up, and I'll let you in on a matter of pack safety." Deegan was a creep, but he'd do anything for clout in the pack. He acted like a dog jonesing for a bone with the possibility that he could use this to elevate his station. It was disgusting.

"Pack safety?"

"Yes, pack safety. You won't be able to tell a soul, but it's of immense importance. It's why I've been gone."

Deegan needed no more convincing. He leaned in, and I braced myself. When our lips connected, his felt hard and alien against mine.

I couldn't help but wonder what a kiss from Nickoli would feel like. Would his lips mold perfectly against mine? Would our bodies melt into one another? Not like this, where I had to force my body into the ground to create as much space between us as physically possible. If this were Nickoli, I would relax my body and lean into him, but here my body was stiff as a board. It was a relief when Deegan finally pulled away from me. I felt nothing for him and knew I never would.

"Now move," I ordered, and thankfully he complied after only asking once. He rolled off me and sat beside me. He wore a strange expression on his face. It seemed to truly puzzle him that I didn't like what had just happened. "You can't tell anyone else in the pack," I repeated. "Just you and Uncle will know."

"What is it?"

"There's a good chance our pack will be attacked next."

"Deegan's anger flared. "We've got to tell the entire pack then!"

He got up and tried to leave the cover of the trees. "No!" I grabbed his wrist to stop him. "I said 'a good chance' and 'could be', no sense raising a false alarm if it turns out I am wrong." Honestly, it probably wouldn't have been that bad of an idea to alert the entire pack, but I didn't want anyone to know the information came from me. I didn't want to be ostracized yet. "If it makes you feel better, you can tell a small group of trusted individuals to be on high alert for a little while. Don't tell them why, just say you've got a gut feeling or something. Head Alpha needs to be the one to give the order."

Deegan puffed up his chest to argue some more.

"Don't," I said in my most commanding voice. "Swear you'll do as I say. I can even tell Alpha that you're in on it, and he can use you for council."

He deflated. "I swear, Little Alpha." He reached down and effortlessly pulled me to my feet.

"Good," I said as I smoothed out my dress. "One more thing. I was never here." He had enough sense not to argue with me as I walked away.

CHAPTER 18

I continued on to Uncle's hut. Had I never been to this pack before, I still would have been able to pick out Head Alpha's hut from amongst the others. In a show of superiority, Head Alpha's hut dwarfed those around it, and embellishments adorned it. While the other huts simply sported the plain off-white color of dried clay, Head Alpha's depicted scenery referencing important events in the pack's history.

I could see Uncle's hut now, but a figure unexpectedly blocked my path. She must have just left one of the nearby huts. Strange that I didn't hear anyone talking. The loose, knee-length tunic she wore was dyed black, and she wore a thin black veil that covered her head down to her shoulders; our traditional mourning clothes. She carried a flower-gathering basket filled with various herbs from the surrounding woods and mountainside. I had no time to hide. She looked up from her basket and promptly dropped it. Sprigs near the basket's opening bounced out and scattered on the well-traveled grass at her feet.

Mother.

Her hands flew to her mouth, and I had to quiet her before she could cry out. The relief on my mother's face broke my heart. She closed the distance between us in what felt like a blink of an eye and crushed me in a hug so tight I could barely breathe.

"Mother." I gasped out. I could feel her tears permeate the veil.

She didn't let go. "Where have you been?" There was a hitch in her voice.

"I-" How could I explain to her? Tears welled in my eyes. I wanted to stay home so badly. The tears spilled onto my cheeks. "Mother, I can't stay here."

"What are you talking about, baby?" She stepped back enough to look at me, but still kept her hands on my shoulders.

Baby, she hasn't called me that in a very long time. I broke down and told her about fleeing the compound. Her expression stayed soft. She cupped my face with her hands and used her thumbs to make small circles on my cheeks, calming me.

"You have done nothing wrong." She reassured me. "You did not run out of cowardice."

"Running is always the coward's choice."

"It most certainly is not." She said sternly. "Who told you that nonsense?"

My eyes darted towards Uncle's hut, and Mother's face darkened. "That man is not god, Leza."

I chewed on my lip while I thought her words over. In the past year, Uncle did seem more withdrawn than he had been before, and it sometimes felt like the pack disinterested him but leading a nation can be stressful. No one is perfect, not even Uncle. Still, I couldn't stop thinking that if he found out that I ran, he would be disappointed in me.

"Mother, there's something I need to tell Uncle, and I have friends waiting for me."

She gave me another quick, hard hug. "I expect you home." I chewed on my lip again. Exasperated, she said, "At the very least, I expect to hear from you!" Her tone left no room for argument. "I love you, Leza."

"I love you too."

CHAPTER 19

I didn't need any more distractions, so I hurried over to Uncle's hut. I crept along the back wall and heard voices from inside by way of a window left cracked open. A bush just to the right under the window provided cover so I could wait for Uncle's guest to leave.

"No, I haven't seen her." I heard Uncle say. He was talking about me. *Who would be asking about me?* I peeked up into the window out of curiosity for a quick look. Uncle's back faced me, but I could still see a bit of his left profile. Notably, I didn't see anyone else in the room with him. He held a bowl in his hands. His head bent over it as if he were talking to his reflection bouncing off the bowl's liquid contents.

"Are you certain?" A voice asked from the bowl. My blood froze. There was no mistaking Majie's voice. I slid back to the cover of my bush; my breath caught in my chest.

"I would never lie to you," Uncle replied with genuine hurt in his voice.

I swore I felt the ground quake, but no one shouted if they felt it too, so it must have just been my world flipping upside down. Uncle is in league with Majie? I didn't want to believe it, but I could almost hear my image of Uncle shatter in my head, ripped apart by this new information. That explains why he wouldn't chase after The Appointed after the attack on the Shilo pack.

"I love -" I heard him start to say but I bolted from my hiding place, not caring if anyone saw me; I just needed to get away from there. My legs pumped as hard and fast as possible to get away.

◆ ◆ ◆

I flew past Deegan, then almost fell coming to an abrupt stop.

He looked confused, but I didn't give him time to speak. "Don't trust Uncle." I blurted out.

"Wha-"

"Don't tell him anything. If they attacked the pack, wake everyone to fight, but don't let Uncle know you know!" I started running again.

"Wait!" He called and gave chase, but I focused on finding a place to teleport back to Nickoli.

After several more yards, I deemed it far enough and hastily shook some of the liquid from the vial. A pentagram immediately formed and glowed as if it could sense my urgency. "Nickoli's house," I said in a shaky voice.

I heard my name called from behind me. I turned to see Deegan, but he rapidly faded from my vision as the grey mist climbed up my body. He reached his hand out for me, but by the time he outstretched his arm, the mist had already engulfed me.

CHAPTER 20

When I registered the world again, I noticed Nickoli and Evander were not where I had left them. They had settled themselves in some wooden lawn chairs in closer proximity to Nickoli's house. Evander lounged back in his chair like he was sunbathing, even though it was too late in the day for tanning.

I took a few steps, then retched again.

"Aw, damn," Evander said, propping up from his relaxed position. The boys got up, but my stomach hadn't stopped rolling yet, so I frantically motioned for them to stay back. "The pill is supposed to make you not do that. Guess I need to work on the formula some more."

Nickoli gave him a horrified look. "You gave her something still in testing?!"

Before Evander could respond, I threw up once more. Both boys looked concerned but backed away to sit back down in their seats, waiting for me to get a handle on myself.

I covered my face with my hands and dissolved into tears. I was so shell-shocked that I didn't know what else to do.

"What's the matter?" Nickoli asked, his voice thick with worry. He approached me anyway and gently guided me away from the pile of sick I had produced and toward his recently vacated chair. I kept my hands plastered to my face. His touch felt like a cool washcloth on fevered skin, but I didn't want to sink into the relief he offered. Once I sat, he released his touch, and I wanted to cry harder, wanting it back, but I didn't want to cause more of a scene, so tried to calm myself.

It took a moment before I could compose myself enough to speak. "I overheard Uncle talking to Majie."

"She was there?"

I shook my head

"Talking to her how?" Evander asked.

"Using magic, speaking into a bowl." I sobbed.

"They have a link then," Evander said gravely.

"What's that mean?" Nickoli asked Evander.

"It means that her uncle is in cahoots with The Appointed."

"I've got to go back! I've got to warn -"

"You're not going back there." Nickoli interrupted me.

I prepared to turn, but he grabbed my arm. I wanted to scream at him to let me go, but then I noticed it—the colors. The world looked bright and shiny, as if repainted in crisp colors. My eyes widened, and the tears stopped flowing. I turned to Nickoli, who wore a similarly bewildered expression. With his free hand, he wiped away the last tear that clung to my cheek. It sparkled like a diamond on his fingertip.

Involuntarily, I felt a calm wash over me as Nickoli and stared at one another. His eyes captivated me. They were the most handsome green I had ever seen, and I never wanted to look away.

I reached for him, but then Evander coughed, interrupting us. Nickoli let go, and the world dulled back to normal, and tears welled up in my eyes once more.

"I'm going back. They need to know that they're in danger!" I said firmly and wiped my eyes.

"You're not going back there," Nickoli commanded.

My anger started to pick back up. "Yes. I am." I challenged.

Nickoli clenched his fists. "No, you're not."

I tensed my muscles, ready to fight, but that's when Evander laughed. "This is all very entertaining, but I don't want to see you two come to blows over this when I have a simple solution."

"What's that?" I asked him, the challenge still lingering in my voice.

"I can send the message for you." He bent down and plucked a blade of grass. He cupped it between both hands, then blew in the space where his thumbs met. His pinkies remained in contact with one another, but he uncupped the rest of his hand to reveal the grass had molded itself to resemble a tiny woman. The grass woman shimmied her shoulders, and I noticed a hint of translucent butterfly wings.

"What is she?" I marveled.

"This is a pixie." Evander explained." "Tell it your message, and they will deliver it." He handed her over to me.

"But how will she know who to give the message to?"

"Think of the intended recipient, and it'll pick up their image from your mind."

I furrowed my brows and thought, not knowing immediately what I should say. I just knew I had to warn them. Maybe Deegan didn't understand me when I tried to warn him. What if he tries to clarify with Uncle?

I concentrated on the image of Deegan and cleared my throat. "Tell Deegan that he mustn't let anyone know he saw me today. Not even Head Alpha." I hoped with all my heart that he hadn't already tried to go speak with Uncle. "Tell him to form a small group to monitor things, but don't let the whole pack know what he's doing." I reiterated, "Not even Uncle." I didn't want to tell Deegan that Head Alpha was in league with the enemy, but I had to give him something, or else he might not listen to me. "Tell him that Uncle isn't to be trusted right now, and I'll explain more the next time I see him, but he has to do as I say for now. Tell him that this message is from Leza." The pixie nodded. Its wings buzzed as it took flight from the palm of my hand. It rose straight up for a couple of feet and then spun. The pixie spun faster and faster, and in a blink, it disappeared.

"And that takes care of the werewolves," Evander said.

"Do you think we can get a vampire?" Nickoli chuckled.

Evander grinned. "Actually, I might know a clan."

Nickoli's face fell. "Oh, no, I was just joking."

"Oh, come on! If we're going to fight The Appointed, we might as well do our best to make the odds even." Evander hooked his arms around Nickoli's shoulders and let him onto the pentagram, sidestepping the pile of vomit.

"Coming?" He asked me.

Cautiously, I stood up and made my way to stand opposite of Nickoli.

Evander poured some of the clear liquid on the ground and said, "To the borders."

CHAPTER 21

We appeared on a rocky plateau. My stomach tightened, and I turned to vomit, but only gagged. Nickoli didn't seem phased at all.

"See, you're getting used to it." Evander teased.

"Ha ha," I remarked. "The less we have to do this, the better." I straightened up, but my legs wobbled. Evander grabbed me by the upper arm to steady me.

"Whoa, take a second to get used to the pressure difference. We're pretty high up."

I looked around and noticed he was right; the sky stretched before us and I could have touched a cloud drifting by.

A mountain peak hid a portion of the sun. While there was still enough light to see, the light wouldn't last too much longer.

Evander took in a big, noisy inhale through his nose. "Ah, crisp." He remarked. A beat later, he said, "Well, that's enough of that!" And pivoted around.

A giant opening stood paces behind us. It seemed almost as if the rock itself was yawning. Light didn't penetrate too far into the opening, and I noticed a chilly draft.

My hand floated up and clutched at the scars on my neck.

Nickoli noticed the movement and piped up to stop Evander from entering the cave. "I really was joking about the vampires."

Without stopping or turning around, Evander replied, "Come now, don't be racists!" And he strolled past the threshold of the mouth.

"Let's go," Nickoli said reassuringly. "Evander wouldn't bring us to bad people."

I stared for a moment after them, then took a big, confident stride into the cave.

Evander walked several paces ahead by now, and I took brisk strides to catch up. He held his left hand palm up, and from it, a glowing orb flickered centimeters above his flesh. This orb produced enough light to see that the ground sloped gently downward and that the path was smooth. Even though my feet were well-calloused, they rejoiced at the smoothness of this terrain.

"Won't they be asleep?" I asked.

"Not all of them," Evander remarked coolly.

I heard something move in the darkness in front of us. Goosebumps sprang up on my arms.

"Someone is always up to keep watch," Evander explained.

We walked on in silence for a few more strides before a hushed shuffling sound came from somewhere behind us. I craned my neck as far around as it would go, but Evander's orb made it hard for my eyes to adjust to the darkness beyond it.

The light encompassed us, which meant at least one of us would have seen someone pass by. No one should have been able to get past us and then be behind us without someone noticing.

I attempted to sniff them out, but because vampires lived here, I could only smell them and rocks.

"How nice. You brought us snacks." A male voice echoed from seemingly every direction in the darkness. "And a pretty snack at that." I felt hot breath on the back of my neck and growled.

Evander looked unphased. "Marlow, take me to Eon." His voice sounded more commanding than I ever thought possible, and he never faltered in his strides further into the cave. I didn't dare leave the light, so I didn't allow myself to freeze with fear.

"He's asleep. Why should I wake him for you?"

"Whatever. I know the way to his chambers. I'll see myself there."

"He wouldn't allow a dog and unnatural in his chamber!"

My eyebrows flew up. Evander had been worried about us being racists.

"That's not for you to decide, Marlow." Boomed a deep male voice. "Evander, light the torches." At this new, unfamiliar voice's request, Evander's orb turned into a ball of fire that shot out in front of us, lighting staggered torches that protruded from either side of the wall.

A man dropped from the ceiling, baring his fangs. He wore a tight black t-shirt and a loose pair of satin pants, and every visible muscle was tensed in displeasure.

"Marlow, bring them to me." The voice ordered.

"This way." He said through his teeth and begrudgingly led us.

◆ ◆ ◆

The cave was much more expansive than the tunnel it had first appeared to be. There were cavities scattered around the space, some open, others covered with beaded strings, a few covered by pieces of cloth, and very few with actual doors. Marlow took us through a series of corridors, the uncovered passages, and led us to an opening covered by a thick oak door.

"Enter." The voice said, but it did not boom around the walls as it did before.

Marlow didn't move, so Evander pushed open the door. What I saw on the other side didn't look as if it belonged to a hole in the rock. It looked like a room straight out of a castle. The room looked grand and lavishly decorated in deep reds. It seems vampires share a certain aesthetic, old and red. A magnificent four-post bed with sheer red cloth hanging over it claimed the centerpiece of this room. He had pulled up the cloth that faced the door, sending ripples across the sheer fabric.

This is where the man waited. He had messy salt and pepper hair and looked to be in his late forties. Silky red covers pooled around his waist, almost like a puddle of blood. Marlow had been right; he had clearly been sleeping.

He wasn't wearing a shirt, which displayed a very nasty, jagged scar that raced from his left shoulder to his heart.

His eyes shocked me. They were red, as all vampires' eyes are, but they retained a softness. The closest I had ever seen a vampire's eyes having warmth in them.

"Marlow, leave." He said, almost politely, but with an undertone that ensured Marlow couldn't refuse the request. Marlow glared at us and then left, slamming the door behind him.

"My apologies. Marlow can be a bit," He paused and searched for the right word. "Temperamental." He smiled and exposed his eloquently shaped, slightly inward curved, pearly elongated canines.

I would have picked "bit of an asshole", but I kept that opinion to myself.

"We appreciate his spirit," Evander reassured him.

"Ah, Evander, you've got that gleam in your eyes. What could you possibly be scheming?"

"Nothing special. Just harmony amongst the races, serving up some long-needed justice, and sprinkling in some revenge for the vengeful." While he talked, Evander casually examined his nails and polished them against the upper breast of his shirt. His demeanor was alarmingly casual.

"I noticed the girl is marked." He noted and shifted those red eyes onto me.

I reached over my shoulder and pulled some loose hair to cover my scars.

"Oh, where are my manners?" Evander fussed at himself. "These are my friends. Nickoli." Nickoli nodded a greeting. "And Leza." I gave a polite but still nervous smile. "Nickoli and Leza, this is Eon."

Eon didn't linger on the greetings. "Do you know who marked you, child?" he asked with that same softness I picked up on earlier.

"A coward," I spat. "He snuck up on me and kept me unconscious." Nothing but malice laced my voice when I spoke of André. I couldn't help but see those descending red eyes, the only vision I had of him. The eyes of André contained everything Eon's didn't. André's eyes were cold, hungry, and mad. Nothing comforting lived in them. Eon could almost pass as a non-blood-sucking creature until he smiled. No denying it after that.

"And what happened to you?" He turned his gaze to Nickoli.

"They overpowered and caught me during an ambush. A witch's spell kept me locked inside of myself, forced to live as a pet." Nickoli's voice was so full of hate, it scared me a little. "My people lulled themselves into a false sense of security, and I can not let that continue."

"Many have staged assaults against The Appointed and failed." He paused and stole a pointed glance at all of us before settling on me. "What would make this time any different from the last?"

"By following their example," I replied. Eon cocked one eyebrow in a perplexed expression. "The races united for a common cause when The Appointed formed, and they have wrought devastation on all of their targets. If the races joined against them, we might stand a chance of beating them. Considering how we've always handled things our own way, I don't think they're prepared for if we fought together. The Appointed is used to us standing divided."

Eon thought for a moment, then stretched and yawned. "You have given me much to think about. Let me consider it, and I will send my answer to Evander."

"Thank you," Evander said, then turned with a motion for us to leave.

CHAPTER 22

Evander waited until we left the cave before he poured the potion and spoke the words to bring us back to Nickoli's house. I'm not sure if it was just paranoia or if there actually were multiple sets of eyes watching us from the dark as we made our way to the exit. No doubt in my mind that Marlow's scowl trailed us from the dark.

We materialized on the etched slab in Nickoli's backyard. The boys quickly sidestepped away from me, but this time, I held it together.

Evander didn't stick around, citing having some people to speak with. He practically shooed us off the slab. "Don't worry," He said, "I'll let you know as soon as I hear from the vampires." Perfectly timed, he dissolved into mist, leaving Nickoli and me standing alone in his backyard.

Nickoli broke the awkward silence. "Well, I guess I should go meet with some friends. Let them know I'm back and see how many want to join us."

"Good idea," I replied. At that, he turned to walk away from me. "Um, Nickoli," He paused. "Be safe, okay?"

He chuckled. "I will. Let Mama know I'll be back soon?"

"Okay."

He headed around the house and down the street.

CHAPTER 23

Nickoli

The few solar-powered street lamps we had were already turning on in preparation for the coming dark. I marveled at every house I passed; how did we convince ourselves that The Appointed weren't a threat to us? If they escalated to kidnapping and staging full attacks on other communities, then we most certainly were not safe. What if, somehow, they had taken Anna instead? And what if they killed more people? I shook my head at my internal monologue. No, I couldn't let that happen.

I was still several yards away from my destination when the door burst open, causing me to jump.

"Nickoli?" He asked in disbelief. "Is that you, mate?" His shoulders had a slight pink hue to them, and sand clung to his legs. He claimed surfing to be the best medicine for any emotional problem, so he must have just come from the beach.

"Yeah, Roonie, it's me."

A huge grin spread across his face. "Crikey, I can hardly believe it." He came to me and clapped a hand on my back. His smile faltered. "I'll be honest. I worried we'd never see you again."

"Me too." I gave a nervous laugh and anxiously ran a hand through my hair.

Roonie ushered me inside. "We all got blindsided by that, mate." I took a seat on his lumpy second-hand couch. Roonie had just moved out on his own, so the place looked fairly sparse. He lived in a one-story, one-bedroom, one-bathroom square house, and he was immensely proud of it. "You should come by next week." He remarked. "Mr. Carston said he'll help me patch and reupholster the couch. It's going to be good as new again."

"I can't wait to see it."

Roonie settled himself in a mismatched chair opposite of me.

"Actually, there was something I wanted to discuss with you," I said. Roonie leaned forward, resting his elbows on his knees. "So you know they attacked one of our supply sites.

"Yeah."

"Well, how long do you think it'll be before they come into town?" Roonie furrowed his brow but didn't say anything. "I can tell you. It won't be that much longer."

Roonie leaned back, rubbing a hand over his face as he thought. "What are you getting at, mate?" He asked.

"What I'm getting at is that we need to be proactive about this. Evander is talking with his people as we speak."

"Evander is in on this?"

I nodded. "And I've got a werewolf girl in on it as well. She sent a message to her people not that long ago."

Roonie looked really confused. "A werewolf girl? Why would a werewolf care about us?"

"Because they took her, too." I let the words hang in the air for a moment before continuing. "For her, it's also about protecting her people."

"Blimey. We can't ignore this, can we?"

"No," I said resolutely.

"Alright. I'll help you; you can count me in."

Relief washed over me. "Thank you, but we'll need more than just us."

Roonie waived my concern away. "I'll talk to some of the fellas."

"Thank you," I said again. I stood up and extended my hand to shake his. "Have everyone meet at my house at six o'clock in the morning." He nodded. "I should get back before Mama worries."

CHAPTER 24

Leza

I ignored the strawberry blonde tail protruding from a nearby bush and made my way back to the house to brush my teeth; more than just the vomiting left a foul taste in my mouth.

As soon as I turned off the tap, I heard a rap at the door, almost as if the person had been waiting for me.

"Anna." I greeted as I opened the door. She wore a sly grin and looked at me knowingly.

"Leza." She had a sing-song way of saying my name. "I have a sneaking suspicion about you and my brother." She pointed a finger at me in mock sternness.

My eyes widened, and a slight flush rose in my cheeks. "What-"

She cut me off. "Don't worry, I'll keep it a secret." And she winked. Before I could come up with anything that would change the subject, her mother called out something from downstairs. "Oh, right. Mama sent me to let you know dinner is ready."

I took my seat at the table, again in the mismatched chair, and waited while Anna helped her mother transfer food from the kitchen to the table. Nickoli's father joined me and smiled warmly in greeting.

Before they finished setting the table, Nickoli's mother fretted about where he was.

"He told me to let you know he was visiting some friends, but he wouldn't be too long and would be back soon," I reassured her. She accepted this, but her brows still furrowed with worry.

The subtle clatter of utensils scraping plates filled the air.

◆ ◆ ◆

"So, what's your family like?" Anna almost blurted out. Her mother shot her a look but didn't stop her from asking the question.

I finished chewing my food before answering. "Well, I have a mother and father but no siblings."

"That sucks," Anna said. "Nickoli teases me, and we fight, but I don't know what I'd do without him." Both of her parents smiled at this.

I just shrugged.

"What do your parents do?" Her father asked.
"My mother is the pack healer. She's quite talented, and my

father is an adviser to Head Alpha. Father is more of a scholarly type."

"Do you have schools?" Anna's mother asked, and her cheeks immediately began to flush. "I mean, what are your schools like?" She stammered a bit. "I'm a teacher."

"We teach our pups to read and write, that there is more to the world than the island, and then we hone the necessary skills of tracking, hunting, and fighting."

Anna's mother nodded at this and picked at her food.

Dinner finished quickly after that. Anna's mother kept shaking her head as if scolding herself.

I put my dishes in the sink, thanked Anna's mother for the meal, and returned to my borrowed room.

I rustled through my clothes, looking for something more suitable to sleep in. I settled on a pair of pants that fit loosely around the legs and a tank top. After I changed, I stood at the dresser mirror, overwhelmed by the sheer amount of flowers I soon had to pick out of my hair.

A knock at the door interrupted that thinking. "It's open," I said, suspecting Anna again. I didn't move away from the mirror and plucked a flower out, hoping she would offer to help.

The door pushed open to reveal, not Anna, but Nickoli.

"I just wanted to let you know I'm home," He said, shifting his weight back and forth from each leg. "Hey, do you need help with that? Anna is always doing something extravagant and then needs help undoing it so I have some experience." He joked.

I looked down at my meager pile of flowers on the dresser, then up to the vast quantity still left in my hair, and nodded.

Nickoli entered the room, sat in the middle of the bed, and patted the space in front of him, signaling for me to come.

I obeyed and sat cross-legged on the plush comforter. Indeed, expertly, he plugged the flowers out, and within minutes he cupped a large pile in his hands. He deposited them on the nightstand and started undoing the braids. My back straightened. Each touch of his finger sent a pleasant tingle down my spine. He ran his fingers through my hair, and my shoulders gave a slight shudder. I anticipated another one, but it didn't come.

My ears grew hot as I felt him staring at the back of my head. Not knowing what else to do, I just turned to face him.

His face held a quizzical expression as if contemplating something. Before I could break the silence and ask him about it, he started reaching for me, cautiously. His hands rose to cup the sides of my face. Just the thought of him immediately consumed me I barely registered the change in color this time when he touched me. His face changed to that same soft expression I saw before. He moved one hand to the back of my neck and started removing the space between us. I closed my eyes and didn't resist. Our lips met, and every one of my senses sang with joy. I knew if I opened my eyes, the colors of the room would be dancing. I threw my arms around his neck and pressed my body into him. He didn't resist me either.

Somehow we both ended up lying side by side. I felt his head pull back, and I opened my eyes. He lightly kissed the top of my forehead, the tip of my nose, and then the scars on my neck.

I hugged him tighter, but involuntarily, and betrayingly, yawned.

"You should sleep." Maybe I was just imagining it, but he sounded disappointed. "We've got a big day ahead of us." He motioned for me to get up, but I twisted my legs around one of his.

"Stay?" I laid my head on his chest, and his heart thudded fervently. "If only for a little longer?"

"Okay." He said, and his fingers began lightly running up and down my spine.

CHAPTER 25

I woke up snuggled under the crook of Nickoli's arm. He laid sprawled out on his back with his mouth slightly agape. I smiled, then gently pressed my lips to his chest and carefully slid out of bed. I grabbed some clean clothes, a tank top, and a pair of shorts, both black, then slipped into the bathroom for a quick shower.

Once refreshed, I brushed my hair and pulled it into a high bun.

Floorboards creaked above me, which meant Nickoli was getting ready. I repacked all of my belongings into my backpack.

Anna's bag of presents still sat untouched on the dresser. I took the clothes out to cram them into the backpack as well. She had bought me two extra dresses; one light pink with ruffles on the skirt and short sleeves, and the other a moss green sun dress. I smiled as I folded them. Anna was a good kid.

Nickoli was tiptoeing down the stairs when I opened up the door. He pressed his index fingers to his lips and cut his eyes over to Anna's door. Quietly, I closed the door and tiptoed after him.

I followed Nickoli into the kitchen, and while he rummaged through the pantry, I used the faucet to fill up my canteens.

Before we left, Nickoli left several pieces of folded-up paper on the counter beside the sink. He positioned it with care so his family couldn't miss it.

Once outside, I felt comfortable enough to whisper. "I need to get in touch with my pack. I have to know if anything has happened."

"Everyone should be here any minute-"

"Please, there has to be some way. I just need to talk to someone."

Nickoli sighed in defeat. "I'll see if Evander is up." He crept back into his house, then returned several minutes later.

I opened my mouth to ask about Evander when I heard his voice speak from behind me.

"My gods, do you realize how early it is?" Evander didn't look as well kept this time with bedhead and a light pullover hoodie and sweatpants, a stark contrast to his suave look of yesterday.

"Don't blame us, you were up." Nickoli teased.

"I'll curse you; I will." Evander quipped back.

"I'm sorry," I butted in. "But I need to check in and make sure my pack is still standing."

The worry in my voice must have been evident because Evander's face softened in response. "Of course you do. Want me to transport you back?" Evander started to fish around in the pouch on the front of his hoodie.

"No," Nickoli interjected. "We don't have time for that. Everyone should be arriving soon."

"Alright, I don't suppose you have a bowl on you, do you?"

"Yes, actually." I produced a shallow bowl from my pack.

"Excellent. Fill it with water." I did so by emptying one of my canteens and then held it out to him. "No, no, you keep it. Now, take a seat and close your eyes. Good. Now take a deep breath in, then release it slowly. Center yourself." As I did so, I could hear him messing with the water, like he was stirring it with his finger. Evander placed a hand on the back of my head. My eyebrows flew up in surprise at the touch. "Don't open your eyes just yet!" Gently, he applied pressure, moving my head forward until the tip of my nose touched the water. "Be careful with your breathing, don't want you snorting any water." I stifled a chuckle and almost inhaled as I did. "Get a clear picture of the person you wish to speak with." The image of Deegan floated into my mind. "You'll appear in the closest body of water closest to this person, so concentrate hard and repeat after me. Hecate."

"Hecate."

"Goddess of magic."

"Goddess of magic."

"Lend me the power to complete this spell."

"Lend me the power to complete this spell."

"For you are the mother of all my magic."

"For you are the mother of all my magic."

"Good. Now open your eyes."

When I did, I wasn't looking into a bowl of water but rather up at a porch ceiling. A very familiar porch ceiling.

"Deegan?" I asked as loud as I dared, which came out as a little more than a whisper.

"Leza?" He answered. "Where are you?"

"Are you on my porch?"

"Yes, but that doesn't answer my question as to where you are."

"In the bowl by the door." His head entered my field of vision as he bent down. "Are we alone? I can't see over the rim."

He lifted his head and looked in every direction. "We're alone." He said. Even in a bowl, I didn't like the context.

"Well, you look intact, so nothing happened last night, right?"

"Right." He confirmed, and relief trickled through my body.

"Will you do me another favor?" I asked.

"Do I get another kiss?" He fired back eagerly.

"No, but you get a fight out of it."

He thought for a minute. "I guess. What's the favor?"

"Gather the group of people you told to be on high alert, pack at least a week's worth of essentials, and start heading north."

"Where are we going? How will we know when we arrive?"

"You'll know because you'll run into me. Remember, don't tell anyone what you're doing, especially Head Alpha." I paused, trying to think of an excuse. "It's a surprise." I managed lamely.

He didn't seem quite sold but replied, "I've already sworn to your secrecy, Little Alpha."

"Alright, prepare yourself, and I'll see you soon."

CHAPTER 26

"I'm done," I announced to Evander once Deegan left my porch.

"Close your eyes," Evander instructed as he placed a palm on my forehead. He paused, then gently guided me up. "You can open them now."

"Thank you, Hecate," I murmured under my breath. It felt like the right thing to do.

Evander yawned dramatically. "Now, if it's alright with you two, I'm going to get a few winks before things get going. See you later." He waved as he retreated, presumably to the pentagram in the backyard.

I heard footsteps approaching from behind me, and I tensed.

"Relax," Nickoli said with a quick squeeze of my hand. "It's just my friends."

Cutting through the yards were five very able-bodied-looking young men. One with olive sun-kissed skin and wavy shoulder-length brown hair half tiptoeing, half sprinting toward Nickoli. Nickoli covered his mouth with a hand to keep himself from laughing. He wrapped his arms around Nickoli in a big, warm greeting as the others caught up to where we stood.

"Leza," Nickoli said as he clasped his friend on the back to disengage from the hug. "This is Roonie."

"Good day." He said politely. "That there is Laz." Laz looked as if he had just smelled something sour. "Lankston." He was the shortest of the bunch. "Price." He had eyes that laughed. "And Dean." Dean had a vibe that vaguely reminded me of Deegan. All but the first nodded in greeting.

"You told me we were going to fight." The first one, Laz, said. "Why is a girl here?"

There is one surefire way to light my short-fused temper, and that was it. I squared my shoulders, sizing him up.

"She's not from here," Nickoli interjected. "Girls aren't as fragile where she's from."

"Sure." Laz scoffed.

"Try me." I challenged as I let my pack slip off my shoulders to the ground.

"I wouldn't want to hurt you, Princess."

Nickoli firmly placed a hand on my shoulder, and I shrugged him off. I would not let the dazzling colors quell this fight. "Oh, I see. You're afraid to get beaten by a girl. Which, just proves that males aren't the superior gender."

The other guys snickered, and Laz's face turned red with anger.

"I think you lost this one, mate." Roonie chuckled.

"We need to get going." Nickoli urged.

I turned to pick up my back off the ground when rushing footsteps informed me of an incoming assault. I pushed my back leg out and caught him just below the chest, sending him flat on his back. I pounced and held him down by the throat with my right hand. "Only cowards attack when their opponent's back is turned." I spat and gave him a nice black eye with my free hand.

I straightened up, released him, and turned back to my pack. Nickoli had picked it up and held it out to me. "Finished?" He asked.

Laz moodily rose back to his feet, his face redder than before. One of the other boys kept him quiet. We were supposed to be sneaking off on our mission, after all. Nikoli's family or nearby neighbors could have easily heard this commotion.

"I think I made my point."

"Then let's go then...before you wake up the entire house."

CHAPTER 27

B y the end of the first night, I could tell that this was going to be a disaster, to put it politely. These boys had no discipline. For the entire day, Laz never transitioned out of his lion state. He huffed and produced billowing groans. It took all my willpower not to march back there and hit him again.

When we reached our first rest stop, I couldn't hide my feelings any longer.

"What is the matter with you all?" I exploded. "Do you think this is going to be easy?" All the boys cast their eyes away from me. "All day, you've done nothing but goof around."

"What's your problem?" Dean asked. He looked over at Nickoli as if to ask him what he was doing with this crazy woman.

"What's my problem?" I reiterated. "My problem is that I'm trying to not die, and hanging around with you all has me seriously questioning our chances of survival."

"There's no need to -" Roonie tried to interject, but I cut him off.

"No need to what? Have you ever faced them?" They all shook their heads. "I have." I gulped as images of the battlefield drifted to the front of my mind. "I know what happens to people when they aren't ready." Although I healed fully after my battle, I vividly remember how battered I was the first time André found me in the woods. "Wrestling moves aren't going to cut it when it's time to fight."

The boys glumly sat down their stuff, but no one argued. Laz, who had been carrying his backpack in his mouth, spat his stuff on the ground and snarled his teeth at me.

The boys looked shocked, but I brightened at the action. "You might be a bit of an ass," I said, "But you also might be onto something. If you all fight in the form of some sort of large predator, then you could handle yourselves with no problem."

Nickoli stood beside me as we watched the boys huddle and converse amongst themselves. One by one, they each picked an animal. A bear, a tiger, a hippopotamus, a crocodile. They transformed back into their normal selves.

"What about you, mate?" Roonie asked Nickoli.

"Don't underestimate the advantage of an aerial attack," Nickoli said and transformed his fingers into talons for emphasis.

That seemed to satisfy the group, and we all settled down for some rest.

CHAPTER 28

Nickoli took the lead, and we pushed ourselves at a good pace. We busted into a clearing, all of us panting and glistening with sweat when Nickoli halted.

"This is it." He indicated. I flopped over, bending at the waist, and rested my hands on my knees. Taking big breaths to match the demand of my lungs. We all surveyed our surroundings and noted that the clearing appeared empty.

"Strange," Nickoli said. "I thought Evander would have beat us here."

"Witches." One of the boys remarked from behind us. Nickoli shrugged his shoulders in response.

Laz dropped his stuff to the ground and flopped down beside them. Since no one would carry it for him, he still had to carry his pack in his mouth.

"Good idea," Dean said and did the same.

"Aren't you ever going to cheer up?" Lankston asked Laz as he, too, sat down.

Laz just grumbled and looked away.

"Aw," Price mocked. "His pride is hurt." No one laughed, and his face hardened in embarrassment.

"It was a good try, Price." Roonie chuckled.

My brows knitted as I thought, and Nickoli noticed. "What is it? " He asked me.

"I'm worried my people might need a little help getting here. I only told Deegan to bring the group north, and that could take them too far to the east or west of here."

"I could fly out and mark the trees to lead them." He suggested.

My face brightened. "That's a fantastic idea!" I gave him a quick kiss on the lips. Short touches like that made it easier to avoid getting lost in the amazing sensation that happens when we touched.

"OoOo." The boys mocked behind us, making kissy noises.

"Shut up," Nickoli grumbled, smiling. Since my back was to the group, I rolled my eyes but grinned, too.

He was turning away from me when I stopped him. "Here, take this with you." I pulled out yesterday's dirty, sweaty tank top from my backpack. I answered Nickoli's question before he could ask. "We know how to use our noses; they know my scent and will have an easier time following marked trees if you use my scent. "

"Makes sense." He gave me a peck on the check and transformed into a red falcon. I held the shirt out, and he grasped it in one foot, let out a brief shriek in goodbye, then flew away to accomplish his task.

I turned to face the group, and Roonie winked at me. I stuck out my tongue to tease him back. We all settled in to wait for Nickoli's return.

CHAPTER 29

We all settled on the edge of the clearing. I laid out Nickoli's long, impractical-looking bag, which he informed me he used to sleep in. He called it a sleeping bag, but I didn't see how it could be comfortable. All the shape-shifter kids had one. Dean explained they used it for camping, but that didn't make too much sense to me either, considering how they lived. They didn't even need to hunt for their food if they didn't want to! Instead of deerskins, they used tarps to keep their sleeping bags dry from the damp ground.

I sat and listened to them hang out with each other. It made me long for my people, people who understood my jokes and anecdotes.

I felt better when Nickoli returned. He drooped my shirt near my mat, changed back into his regular form, and flopped exhausted, face first, on top of his sleeping bag.

Muffled from the material, he said, "I think I did it."

"I'm sure you did an excellent job." I carefully stroked his hair, and he let out a gigantic sigh of relief.

"Wake me up when Evander shows?"

"Of course," I said, and he snored in reply.

CHAPTER 30

Nickoli woke early on his own and harvested some wood for a fire or two.

I was relaxing on my mat when fresh scents in the wind caught my attention. I sat up, tuned to the right, and inhaled deeply. Something familiar mixed in with all the unfamiliar.

I looked up and spotted Evander, along with five others, all flying.
The five strangers rode brooms while Evander stood atop a board wider in the back than in the front and sported rounded ends. He rested his hands in his pockets and his body had adopted a slouchy, relaxed stance.

He smoothly landed and hopped off his board. As he picked the board up, it shrank to about four inches, and he stuck it in his back pocket.

"Eager to see me?" Evander asked, raising an eyebrow.

"You just smell, is all." I teased and wrinkled my nose.

"My heart!" Evander exclaimed while performing a dramatic display of chest pains.

"Evander, stop embarrassing yourself!" A woman tsked as she walked over. "Hi, I'm Sage." She stuck out her hand for a shake. If Evander were a woman, he would have been Sage. They stood at the same height, had the same brown hair and hazel eyes, the same button nose, the same ivory skin complexion, everything.

I stood up and shook her hand. "I'm Leza."

Dean cooly walked over. "Hi there." He greeted with a husk to his voice. "I'm Dean."

A man with blond hair came over and laced his fingers through Sage's. "And I'm Liam." He said with confidence.

Dean's shoulders sagged slightly. "Oh, hey." He said with less enthusiasm.

"Evander?" Nickoli called out as he emerged from the woods behind us, carrying an armful of chopped wood. I almost allowed myself to wonder how he cut it, but then I remembered his unique black potion.

Nickoli deposited the wood by my mat and walked over, dusting off his hands. "Hello, Sage. Is this your fiancé Evander told me about?"

She nodded and beamed a bright smile.

"Liam." Dean filled in.

"Who else did you bring?" Nickoli asked Evander.

"We have Mabel." A plain woman in her twenties meekly waved. "Irene." A woman with choppy, short black hair and sharp features cocked an eyebrow. "Abril." A round, jovial woman waved excitedly. "And Candence." A woman with sad eyes timidly upturned the corners of her mouth into a smile.

Dean meandered over and introduced himself to the women two at a time.

"What about the vampires?" Nickoli continued.

"We only get Alec and Dana," Evander said, not hiding his disappointment. "Those were the only two who share our opinion of The Appointed and how to deal with them. Eon wouldn't force anyone to fight who didn't intent to."

"Well, it's better than nothing." Sage assured.

CHAPTER 31

"W

ell, what should we do now?" Sage asked. Everyone stood around, waiting for the next set of instructions.

Evander spied all of our equipment laid out. "Why don't we get situated?" He suggested.

"Good idea." Sage agreed, and all the witches started digging around in their pockets.

"Where's all their stuff?" I leaned over and whispered to Nickoli.

He chuckled. "Just watch. Evander wouldn't go anywhere without the comforts of home."

"I can hear you." Evander sang back at us. "Why would I rough it when the comforts are so easy to transport?" He pulled what looked to be a white napkin and some toothpicks out of his pockets. He promptly bent down and began to fiddle with it.

I know they can use magic, but this looked ridiculous, and I couldn't hold back a giggle. Evander was a tall man, and his tent was only a few inches tall.

He stood up and cocked an eyebrow at me.

"Sorry," I said, covering my grin with my hands.

"I think you will be." He teased and snapped his fingers. The tent grew full size. Evander motioned me to come over and held the flap open. I peeked my head inside.

A plush-looking queen-sized bed topped with a plump, dark grey comforter immediately caught my eye. A soft, shaggy carpet covered the floor. Dimly lit candles hung from the ceiling, setting a relaxing mood.

My mouth gaped open.

"Told ya," Evander said, elbowing me playfully.

All the witches brought similar setups.

"Anyone in the mood for pictures?" Liam asked.

"What are pictures?" Roonie answered.

"Wildly entertaining," Liam said. "Who wants to build a fire?"

"I will," I answered.

"Excellent, go grab your potions."

I laughed. "You don't need a potion."

Both the shapeshifters and the witches looked at me quizzically. "Just watch." I gathered a small pile of chunky wood and a couple of sticks and picked a centralized spot before getting to work. I made it as small as possible. "We'll have to keep an eye on this," I said out loud. "We don't need to set the whole clearing on fire." I set the chunky pieces of wood up in a teepee shape, then rubbed the sticks together. It didn't take long for it to spark. "Viola, fire," I said.

One by one, the witches took turns turning the flames into pictures, hence the name, and we voted on whose picture looked the best.

I thought Mabel's picture was the best. Her hands whipped skillfully around the fire and sculpted a woman in great detail, then made her dance. The attention to detail was so masterful you could see the flame woman's hair and dress whirl as she twirled playfully. Even Laz turned back into his human form to enjoy the magic.

◆ ◆ ◆

After the witches were done, I felt the need to demonstrate my fighting skill. Making fire the old-fashioned way isn't enough to show off for me. Especially since the shifters could change anytime they wanted, and the witches had their magic; I felt a little insignificant and wanted to shine.

"Hey, Roonie," I called. "Which one of you is the best fighter?"

"Oh, Nickoli. Without a doubt." He replied.

I turned to Nickoli and leaned in close to whisper. "How do you feel about a rematch? One without you being under a spell and me with full blood supply; you up for it?"

"I'm tired." He said unconvincingly.

"I walked just as far as you did." I retorted.

"I don't want to hurt you."

Nickoli was the only person I would allow to say something like that without something getting broken immediately after. "Don't worry, I won't be the one hurting," I smirked.

Reluctantly, he stood up to face me.

"There's a good boy," I muttered, and he scowled mockingly. This was going to be fun.

"No headshots," I said.

"And no groin." He added.

A loose circle formed around us. "You two ready?" Runny asked.

"As I'll ever be," I answered, and backed up several paces. Nickoli nodded and took up a defensive position.

"First one to tap out loses," Roonie announced before signaling for us to begin.

For a moment, nothing happened. The both of us just stared at each other, sizing the other one up, then Nickoli rushed toward me.

At the last possible second, I spun to my left to dodge him, grabbed his wrist, placed my other hand between his shoulder blades, and prepared to yank hard enough to let him know going easy on me wasn't a choice.

Nothing could prepare me for the sensation that slammed into me—as if something had thrown me into the side of a mountain. I had prepared my mind for the colors and feeling of awe and felt confident in my ability to focus enough to ignore them, but I hadn't ever considered this.

When our skin connected, the colors brightened, but this time it felt different. The awe still lingered, but this time it intermingled with sadness. Something inside of me did not approve of us fighting, even just for fun, and was sobbing. Once I identified the feeling of sadness, the bright colors changed into hues of grey and deep blues.

I tried not to reveal any physical sign of my mental shift, so I continued with my plan to yank on his arm and attempted to keep my emotions in check.

As Nickoli twisted his body to gain control and prepare for a counter, I could feel the sobbing presence draining my energy. When Nickoli turned, I could see grief in his eyes, but he must have anticipated that something like this could happen because he took advantage of the strange situation and shoved me to the ground.

Once I fell away, and all contact with him had severed, the emotions vanished as if never present.

Feeling normal again, I scrambled to all fours, facing him. I grabbed his ankles and pulled, making him topple over. I sprang on top of him and we grappled with each other. The feeling came back, but this time I was ready for it, so it hit me with less intensity, but the presence inside of me producing these emotions was not happy.

It didn't take long for me to feel completely exhausted. I struggled out of his hold and shakily stood while he stayed on the ground.

I attempted to find a better, more stable stance, but my legs buckled, and I dropped to my knees.

"Enough," Roonie said. I looked around and noticed the clear, uncomfortable vibe emanating from the spectators. "Let's just call this a draw, yeah?" Both Nickoli and I nodded.

"Must have been more tired than I thought," I said, trying to save face as I made my way over to my mat.

I plopped down on it and my body melted in relief, and I closed my eyes. Shortly after, I felt a presence beside me, and when he caressed my hand, I didn't need to waste anymore more energy to turn my head to look at him, but I did anyway.

He was lying on his back on top of his sleeping bag and looked just as exhausted. He had his eyes closed, but he kept his hand on mine. Whatever feeling from before must have been placated because when he touched me, it shifted back to bright colors and good feelings.

"I got to say," I whispered. "I didn't expect that."

He opened one eye to look at me and made a grunt in agreement, then closed his eyes again. "Doesn't laying like that hurt your neck?" He asked

"Right now, it doesn't matter," I answered, then closed my eyes while I waited for my energy to replenish.

Before I could completely succumb to rest, I heard someone approaching me. It was Candence.

She meekly smiled and whispered, "Hi."

"Hi," I whispered back.

She pointed to Nickoli's and mine touching hands. "That's amazing, you know?"

My eyebrows lifted in astonishment. "You know about the colors?"

She smiled softly. "I work with energy and can see your connection. It's very rare, and you're lucky. It means you two are made for each other. Rest now." She said and shuffled away.

CHAPTER 32

I never fully went to sleep. I just laid there motionless, letting every muscle relax for as long as possible. Nickoli removed his hand some time ago, and though I could still smell him, I wasn't sure if he was still lying beside me or if he had snuck off somewhere else as I thought I heard the grass rustle not long after he removed his hand from mine.

The time without his touch didn't feel as restorative as with it, but I kept my eyes closed all the same.

Maybe I had gotten too relaxed because my eyes flew open at the sound of commotion from people in the camp. Another group had entered the camp. I should have been able to hear their approach, not caught off guard like that. I jumped up, ready to attack if necessary, but immediately relaxed once I recognized who it was.

"Deegan," I called out, both as a greeting and to let the others know the newcomers were allies. Everyone relaxed.

Deegan entered the camp along with five others from our pack.

I walked over to them, and Nickoli and Evander fell in step with me. One flanked my left, and the other flanked my right.

"This is Nickoli and Evander." I introduced. Deegan puffed up, but I pressed on so he couldn't embarrass me. "And this is Ethan, Hunter, Abby, Belén, and Cailyn." I pointed each out to

Nickoli and Evander. All werewolves grew up highly muscled from all the training and the lifestyle we led. All but Cailyn, who glared at me, nodded in greeting.

Cailyn was one of the girls in the pack that would turn into a puddle if Deegan so much as glanced in her general direction. It honestly surprised me to see her keeping her composure. Amongst the girls my age, Deegan alone is as desirable as any young man his age with the title of Head Alpha. To Cailyn, I'm an obstacle that needs to be taken down.

Cailyn shifted her eyes from me to Evander, then to Nickoli. Evander appraised her like the other girls—it seemed boys will be boys, no matter where they are from—and she waved cutely at him in response, dipping her chin to look up at him through her lashes. She then turned to Nickoli and winked. Involuntarily, I started to growl, but it turned into a cough when I realized what I was doing. Cailyn didn't fall for it and grinned mischievously.

I was not looking forward to the time I was going to have to spend with her.

"Deegan," I began, and Cailyn scowled, "There's a lot I need to fill you in on. Come on." I motion for him to follow me to a more private section of the clearing.

CHAPTER 33

I t felt like night purposefully evaded us for as long as possible, though it fell a few hours after others from my pack arrived. By the time it finally arrived, I was mentally exhausted.

Because of my reaction, when Cailyn flirted with Nickoli, she would not leave him alone. Nickoli acted indifferently toward her, but it took a huge toll on me to avoid reacting every time she attempted to hang onto him. Nickoli would politely, but firmly, shrug her off, but it wouldn't be long before she found an opportunity to brush his arm with her hand as she walked by or playfully slap him on the arm when someone said or did something funny.

If Cailyn ultimately wanted Deegan, it would be her just desserts to have this entire farce blow up in her face later on. If I were Deegan, this show of pettiness would be a turnoff for me. But I'm not Deegan, and you could tell all the attention Nickoli received made him extremely jealous. Deegan wouldn't leave ten steps from my side. On second thought, maybe Cailyn and Deegan were perfect for each other.

Thankfully, when the vampires arrived, it provided me with a chance to get away from Deegan. No matter how tough you think you are, everyone will act wary when a vampire is around.

Even though Evander told us only two would come, it disappointed me when no one else arrived with them. I had secretly hoped they rallied more people for our cause on their way to meet us. Evander introduced the man as Alec and the woman as Dana. They both stood as still as stone and their eyes drank in every face of our party.

Alec was a short, squat man who looked to be 30, and Dana was a tall, slender woman who could have been anywhere between 15 to 25 years old, though being vampires, they were certainly much older than they both appeared to be.

"It's so they know who's on their side," Evander explained when he noticed my uneasiness.

They looked over his face last, then turned to walk away.

"Wait, where are they going?" I asked.

"To hunt," Evander said. "Just to be safe." He gave a nonchalant shrug. "Excuse me." He snapped off a small branch from a nearby tree and mumbled over it.

The branch vibrated in response. Evander knitted his eyebrows, and the branch grew six inches. Mabel walked over, grabbed Evander's hand, then began silently moving her lips. Evander dropped the branch, and it grew to roughly six feet in length and shot up to three feet in height. Its width widened out to look as if it could house two people laying shoulder to shoulder. Evander placed a hand on the side of it for a moment before tipping it to reveal its completely hollow interior.

"Thanks," Evander told Mabel. "Everything must have drained me more than I thought today. I'll have to take a rejuvenating draft."

I stared, stunned.

Reading my face, Evander said, "For when the sun rises. It's not a pretty sight." He shuddered dramatically.

CHAPTER 34

A mellow mood settled over the group.

"Just to double check," Evander thankfully interrupted Cailyn during another one of her stories no one found interest in. "This is everyone, correct?"

"Yup." I answered, grateful to be pulled away.

Evander stifled a yawn. "I think I'm going to hit the hay." He said, gazing longingly at his tent.

I wasn't familiar with the expression, but I understood the meaning. "Good idea. We can establish a plan of action after we all rest." I took a quick head count; twenty, plus the two vampires we hadn't seen since. "Hey, can we trust the vampires to keep guard or should we split into watches? Groups of four should be enough to keep things even and we can draw sticks to–"

Evander cut me off. "I'm going to stop you right there." His tone was so serious that it surprised me. "I simply can not function on anything less than seven hours of sleep, and that's pushing it." My eyes rolled in response; I should have known he can't be serious. "I have a better idea and we'll get some decent shut-eye." He cleared his throat. "Witches," He called. I couldn't hide my look of amazement; Evander could actually muster a commanding tone. "Please, join me in creating a safe place to sleep." With humor in his tone, "I can't speak for anyone else, but

I never mastered sleeping with one eye open." That elicited a chuckle from the werewolf group who actually had been trained to maintain alertness even while sleeping.

Each witch fanned out, creating a loose circle around our camp facing outward. They held their arms down at their sides with their fingers splayed out. Starting with Evander, he let out a low baritone "om". The witches repeated the sound in a round of different octaves until they melded into harmony as the last witch joined her voice. The harmony lasted for another breath. They clapped their hands simultaneously and fell silent.

A shimmering inked from all their fingertips which rose and expanded to meet the boundaries of the other witches. We all watched in awed silence.

A dome formed around us. The witches stood there for a moment, then collectively let out a breath.

"Good night, everybody." Evander called out unceremoniously and promptly retreated to his tent.

"What does that do?" Abby marveled aloud. Werewolves only really know the potions peddlers bring around to trade occasionally. No one in my group had ever seen anything like that.

Irene's situated herself on a wicker stool outside her tent door after the spectacle.
"This will wake all of us if any non-allies approach." She answered with a smile.

"Cool." Abbey breathed the word.

I made my way over to my mat and got situated for sleep.

When I laid my head on my small pillow, I breathed in the familiar scent of home, but an unfamiliar scent caught my attention as well; one that reminded me of spring. Curious, I turned to investigate the unfamiliar scent. Irene, who settled her things close to where my pack had set up, dabbed herself with some sort of perfume.

Simply knowing where the scent was coming from didn't sedate my curiosity. "What is that?" I asked her.

"I call it Essence of Fresh." She smiled as she quickly touched behind both of her ears. "You simply dab it on and it'll combat the offensive odors. Like you've taken a bath! Would you like some?" She extended the little bottle to me. I sat up, shrugged, then took it. I've endured two days of heat and sweat, it couldn't hurt to freshen up a bit.

After some dabs myself, I felt more relaxed. I sighed and handed the bottle back. In the morning, I'll have to remember to ask about purchasing a bottle for myself.

"Makes you feel better, doesn't it?" She stated it more than an actual question as she put the bottle away.

I nodded and settled back into sleep's familiar embrace.

CHAPTER 35

André

André walked over to where the portrait of Maria hung and gingerly took it down. The frame felt solid in his hands, but he cradled it as if it were a bird's egg. How long had it been since he held her like this? Too long.

André brought the portrait close and inspected every centimeter, making sure no stain remained. Had the oils dulled or had it always looked like this? *"I must find someone to restore this."* He thought to himself and placed her lovingly back on her hook, where she belonged.

He closed the door then, stepping over glass pieces, pillows, and the overturned coffee table, André trudged his way over to the loveseat and flopped down. He hung his head down and sighed. This was a disaster. Majie had become too unfocused. Time to take matters back into my own hands. Supposedly, humans on the mainlands don't believe in vampires anymore. He mussed to himself.

This sparked an idea and he snapped my head up. The humans would be easy prey. He could go back there himself and wreak havoc on those monstrous beings. André grinned, exposing his fangs.

Arranging for transport would be the troublesome part. He frowned. Majie might not let me go so easily.

He still had a long day ahead of him. *"Perhaps a plan will come to me after I get some rest,"* He thought as he walked back over to his coffin.

CHAPTER 36

Leza

I woke with a start for no particular reason. I sat up and looked around. No one else seemed disturbed and continued to rest peacefully, which meant nothing had disturbed our protection barrier. Nickoli had placed his sleeping bag so close to mine they touched, and he lay peacefully beside me. I allowed the smile that snuck onto my lips to linger as I looked at him.

I tilted my head up toward the moon. My smile widened as I gazed at it; a waxing moon always excited me.

A frown gradually replaced my smile. I blinked hard once in confusion, thinking my eyes had played a trick on me, but they hadn't. The image of the moon subtly rippled in the sky. As I watched, the rippling left the moon and started descending toward me. The rippling changed into a billowing pale white fabric and a pair of arms and a face revealed themselves from under the cloth.

I attempted to growl or yell, but no sound came out. It was Majie. When sound didn't work, I attempted to move, but her gaze kept me rooted.

The look on her face could have been mistaken for serene had it not been for her eyes. Cold, dark, and calculating.

She turned her gaze to Nickoli, and I felt my body forced up. A sly smile appeared on her deceivingly innocent face when she turned back to me. She placed a slender finger over her lips. Her eyes blazed with such intensity, every muscle in my body felt immobile. She removed the finger from her lips and touched the tip of my nose.

With that, I felt all the air knocked out of me and replaced with hot, searing pain.

I knew this feeling, but pain is not something that usually accompanies my transformations. My bones screamed, and my clothes tore while my body morphed. Every fiber of my being yelled out to the word 'unnatural'.

When the full moon rises and a wolf transforms, the feeling can only be described as right, not a sensation that causes you to writhe.

An agonizing howl erupted from me. To her surprise, my howl echoed across the sleepy camp. A rock sailed through the air toward her, but passed right through her form, breaking the spell as she disappeared.

◆ ◆ ◆

I fell back to the ground, seizing as my confused body reverted to its human form.

When my body stopped convulsing, I registered Nickoli hovering protectively over me, using his sleeping bag to cover my now-naked body while Sage rummaged through my pack behind him. She quickly pulled out some articles of clothing. Sage pulled on my more intimate garments, then swiftly and gently tugged me into a shirt and pair of pants.

Once clothed, Nickoli dropped his sleeping bag and started fretting over me. "What just happened?" He asked while Sage shook Irene awake.

"Majie." I gasped out. My insides were still unsure of where they needed to be. "How is everyone still asleep?" I asked.

Sage and Irene shared a quick hushed word together before joining us. Irene held another tiny bottle in her hand.

"What do you mean?" Sage gently asked.

"Didn't you hear me?" I desperately looked between the two witches.

Sage looked confused. "Hear you?"

"What woke you up?" I asked, equally confused.

"I was hit with a rock." She rubbed the small red circle on her forehead.

I looked over at Nickoli. "Did you - " I didn't have to finish my question because he was already nodding.

"I threw the rock." He looked over at Sage. "Sorry."

"That's what I get for leaving the flap open." She teased like a sister would her brother.

"I think I have something for it." Irene offered. "Here." Irene handed me the small bottle. "Drink all of it. Sage told me what happened. This should make you feel right again." I up-ended the bottle without hesitation. As the liquid slid down my throat, the lingering pain immediately dissipated. My head cleared, and I steadied myself.

Suddenly, everyone around us bolted upright, waking instantly, and Sage and Irene stiffened. Seemingly at the same time, Alec and Elizabeth appeared, both of their eyes appearing bright and fresh.

The rest of the camp stirred as Alec explained: "Creatures are approaching."

"We've already taken three," Elizabeth informed as she wiped a stain off of her porcelain cheek.

"They come from three sides. Our kind is amongst them; be prepared." And just as quickly as they appeared, the two vampires bolted.

Everyone was up and moving by then. We quickly packed and piled our supplies into a spot we could only hope would be out of the way, then gathered in the middle of the clearing, forming a loose circle; the best defensive position against a multiple-sided attack.

The cracking of low-burning fires and the anticipation-filled breathing of those around me were the only sounds breaking the silence. Adrenaline pulsed through my entire body, sharpening my senses. A nervous energy bubbled up from my stomach, banishing any exhaustion I felt from my previous ordeal.

Faint sounds of crunching grass and snapping twigs caught my attention. They came from the north, south, and east. All of us werewolves focused our attention on those three directions, and everyone else followed suit.

Nickoli transformed into his falcon form and the other shapeshifters followed his lead, transforming into their respective animal forms.

A shadow emerged from the tree line. Her red eyes shone from the dark and fixated on me.

I sucked in air as she ran toward me. Absently, I noted other figures bursting from the tree line.

I crouched. The only hope you have when fighting a vampire is to use their own strength against them.

As she got closer, she smiled so sinisterly that I would have shivered with fear without the adrenaline already claiming my body.

At the last moment, Nickoli, positioned to my left, launched himself into her. She had focused so tightly on me, she didn't see his attack coming and crashed to the ground following impact.

I desperately wanted to help Nickoli, but I couldn't because another figure ran toward me from my periphery.

I whirled around in a defensive crouch and bared my teeth. I involuntarily choked back a snarl before it left my throat as my mind processed my new assailant.

The man didn't stop. In fact, he seemed to speed up with rage when I turned to face him.

"Un- " Swiftly, his left knee connected with my stomach. The force knocked me back. The earth felt cold and hard. My head snapped back and thwacked on the grass. " - cle!" The last syllable of the word left as a wheeze with no air left in my lungs.

Stars swam through my vision and my head rang like a bell.

He tsked. "You know better, Leza. Always keep your guard up in a fight."

Disoriented and coughing, I stared up at him. Was he mocking me? I rolled on my side to conceal the treacherous tears welling in my eyes and attempted to compose myself.

Uncle had been my biggest role model throughout my life. A man I looked up to and admired more than my own father. I thought I drained all my tears for him when I first discovered his betrayal, but apparently not. Memories of sparing, fishing, and years of advice flooded my thoughts and with each wave, another tear fell. Uncle stood before me now as my enemy.

His decisions hurt my heart. Decisions I knew wholeheartedly the council would have advised against—if he even bothered to consult them.

I finally stopped coughing. "Why?" I wanted to wail, but I needed to keep some dignity. I forced out a cough to even out my voice and sat up, wiping tears from my cheeks. "Uncle, why are you doing this? Why have you given your allegiance to her?" Memories of our sister pack's slaughter erupted in the forefront of my mind. Rage burned in my throat. Our people died for nothing! Why defend our sister pack if he sided with the enemy the whole time?!

I stood up a little too quickly. The earth rocked, but I kept my ground in front of him. "She killed our people!" I spat at him. My face felt red and hot. "She killed our kind!" My fist balled up. "You were supposed to protect us and yet you're killing us!" With anger fueling me, my fist shot out on a direct path to his face. He caught my wrist before I could connect with his teeth. I felt a pull in my shoulder socket as he spun and flung me back into the dirt.

"Stop this nonsense." He crouched behind me to get on my level as I pulled my knees from under me. "We can go home now and no one in the pack has to die." His voice sounded soothing, attempting to persuade me into leaving the field.

For a beat, I fell silent. Grunts, screams, and heavy breathing filled the surrounding space. "No one should have to die in the first place!" I sprang up on all fours and donkey-kicked him in the face, catching him off guard. His head snapped back and blood bubbled out of his nose.

Hurriedly, I scrambled to my feet and took a defensive position. I laced my voice with acid. "I'd rather die than be a part of her bat-shit crazy Appointed."

The next few seconds passed in slow motion as Uncle rolled his head forward. His eyes looked animalistic. He scrunched his nose and snapped his teeth together. "That can be arranged." He exploded off the ground and to his feet. I flinched back in fear. He looked pissed and closed the gap between us faster than he should have been able to. I faked a dodge to the left, then crouched to sweep his feet. He had too much momentum and couldn't counter my attack and thus fell face-first into the grass. For a moment, he screamed into the ground, almost throwing a tantrum. He threw himself onto his back and threw himself back on his feet. Fluidly, as if I hadn't knocked him onto the ground a moment ago, his right foot shot out and connected with my stomach. I started to fall, but before I even land, he pounced for me. His hands clasped around my throat and pinned me on my back, straddling my hips to keep me on the ground. I couldn't even gasp for breath because of his tight grip.

My fingers dug into the earth. I pulled up a hand full of dirt and flung it into his eyes. That loosened his grip, so I started bucking around widely, trying to take advantage of this opening. It was enough to dislodge myself from under him.

Moving through my coughs, I whirled to my feet to face him. He looked unsteady as he wiped the dirt from his eyes.

I kicked hard into his right knee and heard a snap. He fell, screaming.

I caught him by the chin and then placed a hand on either side of his face. Without hesitation or further thought, I twisted, hard. Snap.

CHAPTER 37

The snap of Uncle's neck seemed to echo across the clearing. Everyone froze in place. I released his head, and by the time Uncle's body thunked on the ground, the enemy started retreating. Without a leader, they didn't know what to do.

Once the sounds of their running footsteps in the distance went silent, I tore my eyes away from Uncle's body. I didn't want to move, but I couldn't stay physically near him, either.

I saw the haggard group of our survivors, and my feet started taking me toward them.

The scene looked eerily familiar to how it all began. Here I was, bruised and beaten, but alive.

"Leza." A familiar voice called out to me. I turned to see Nickoli limping toward me.

"Nickoli!" Relief washed over me and I turned my stumbling body toward him.

"His eyes scanned me from head to toe. "Are you alright?" He asked. "You're holding your arm differently." He fussed.

"I'll be alright." I laid my head on his chest, and he wrapped his arms around my waist. Our connection zapped some energy through me and I felt both of our bodies relax a little.

I noticed a dark bloodstain on Nickoli's pant leg. "That looks bad. Are you going to be alright?" I asked, fussing over him this time.

"I'll be alright." He reassured with a small smile.

I slipped an arm around his waist and we supported each other on our way to meet with the rest of the group.

◆ ◆ ◆

A gut-wrenching yell erupted from the far side of the clearing. Both Nickoli and I turned and noticed Mabel standing over a limp form on the ground. We hurried over as fast as we could to discover the body belonging to Irene.

She had been small in stature, but she looked even smaller now. Everyone knew her as quiet and kind. She didn't deserve this.

She was lying on the ground like a marionette doll whose strings had been cut. Her eyes stared lifelessly into the distance, wide and glossy, and blood stained the corner of her mouth.

Evander appeared beside me. "Oh, no." He practically whispered. "They're family." Tears welled and spilled onto his cheeks. Sage cautiously approached Mabel. She placed a hand on her shoulder and Mabel jerked. Sage made quiet, calming sounds, and turned Mabel away from Irene's body. Sage gently guided Mable's head to her shoulder, and Mabel succumbed to the comforting embrace.

More cries mingled with Mabel and not all of them originated from the small group of witches standing around us. I looked around and saw two more distinct groups.

My stomach sank.

Nickoli started pulling me toward the shifter group, his injured leg almost forgotten in his hurry.

When reached them, the boys looked stony and choked, gurgling noises came from the ground.

"No!" Nickoli screamed. It came from Roonie. He coughed up a sizeable bubble of blood. Nickoli knelt and frantically looked him over. "Where are you hurt?" Nickoli asked, but Roonie couldn't answer. "I don't see any wounds." Nickoli's voice shook. He scooped up Roonie's head and laid him in his lap. "Hold on. Hold on, okay?" Roonie's eyes became unfocused and lolled around. "Evander!" Nickoli screamed, but Roonie's eyes had stopped moving. "Evander, please!" Roonie's chest gave one last shaky heave and never rose again.

Laz' sniffled loudly. I looked up and all the boys had tears running down their faces. Evander ran over, but it was too late.

Nickoli jostled Roonie's lifeless head. "Roonie, wake up. You need to show me your re-upholstered couch next week, remember?"

I locked eyes with Evander, trying to express everything that had just happened without speaking aloud.

I crouched down beside Nickoli. "Nickoli," I said softly. He didn't answer me. Gently, I touched his face and made him look at me. His sadness hit me like a ton of bricks, and I wanted to crumble beneath it, but he needed me to be strong. "Nickoli," I repeated, "you need to get up now, okay?" I slid Roonie off of his lap and gently tugged him to his feet.

"Coli," was all Evander said before embracing him with a big hug. To me, he said, "I think I can find something to take the edge off. For all of us." I nodded. To Nickoli he said, "Come with me. We've set up a nurses' station. Let's go over there, yeah?" Nickoli didn't answer, but let Evander lead him away. The other boys somberly followed.

CHAPTER 38

I stood there for a moment, at a loss for what to do. How could I comfort him? I turned to follow them, but realized I hadn't seen anyone from my pack. I whirled around and released a sigh of relief when I saw Deegan and some of the others standing around. They all stared at me. My ears started to burn as I made my way over. They were whispering amongst themselves. Why did this feel so strange?

Cailyn sat on the ground, jaw clenched. Something didn't seem right with her right knee.

I felt guilty for the sigh of relief I breathed; all my people made it out alive.

I looked at each of their faces and couldn't read their expressions. No one issued any kind of greeting.

In unison and without saying a word, each member placed their right fist over their heart. The people standing all knelt. All except Deegan.

Solemnly, Deegan said, "Head Alpha," then he, too, placed his fist over his heart and knelt.

My heart slammed into my chest. I took an involuntary step backward. Head Alpha? I couldn't be. I couldn't get enough air into my chest.

"Leza?" Deegan asked.

Abby came to my side. She placed a hand between my shoulder blades and made quick circular motions.

"What's the matter with you?" Ethan asked with disgust in his voice. "Head alpha is supposed to be the strongest of us."

"Shut up." Abby snapped with venom in her voice. "There hasn't been a fight to the death for the Head Alpha position in a very long time." She looked at me and softened her tone. "Plus, the whole pack knows how much Leza loved her uncle."

Abby's understanding comforted me more than I expected. I controlled myself and held up a hand for her to stop, which she did immediately. I looked hard at Ethan. "Are you stupid?" I asked him.

"No." He puffed up.

"You're *seriously* trying to tell everyone here that you'd be able to kill your most beloved family member unaffected?"

"Whatever." He said, and I rolled my eyes. At least I knew without a doubt I could kick his ass if he tried something stupid. I shifted my attention to Cailyn.

"What happened?" She wouldn't answer; she just sat there, continuing to clench her jaw.

"We think her knee is shattered," Abby answered for her, and Cailyn nodded curtly.

"The witches are administering first aid. I'm sure they'll have something for your pain, then we can figure out how to get you back to my mother." I addressed the group. "We need to move her."

"I got her," Deegan said and scooped her into his arms, keeping her injured leg on the outside so he wouldn't accidentally touch it. She yelped a little as he lifted her.

"Once she gets some pain relief, I'm sure she's going to love that he picked her up." I thought to myself, as we made our way over to everyone else as a group.

CHAPTER 39

The witches separated people into groups based on their injuries. Scrapes, bumps, and bruises in one group, bleeding cuts in another group, and severe injury in the last group.

For scrapes, bumps, and bruises, they passed around and administered a soothing salve. It dulled the pain and aided the healing process, but not immediately. Everyone ended up needing that.

For bleeding cuts, they poured a green-tinted potion over the affected area. The bleeding would stop, and the skin would mend, forming an angry red line that received some salve before the injured person walked off.
Unfortunately, the witches didn't have the supplies to handle Cailyn's injury. They gave her some kind of milk-colored potion, but thick in consistency. Within seconds, her jaw relaxed.

Deegan gently sat her down. "I need two straight sticks and something to bind with." He addressed the group. I searched the small firewood pile and found two sufficient pieces for the job. Even though they were a little short, they should still work. Liam produced a thin white sheet.
"Uh, I need to rip this, okay?"

"Do what you got to do," Liam replied.

Deegan took the sheet into his hands and began ripping strips from it. Cailyn giggled drunkenly from her spot on the ground.

He placed the wood on either side of her wounded knee and used the strips to set the wood in place tightly. "That will at least keep it stable, but we need to get her somewhere."

"My mother will know what to do." I chimed in.

"Leza, that's too far of a walk. There's no way–"

I put my hand out and stopped him. "The witches can get her home in mere minutes."

Evander brought Nickoli over to me. He seemed a little better but extremely quiet. I grabbed his hand and channeled all the comforting energy into him.

"I'll get that set up," Evander said, and left to retrieve the supplies from his tent.

"What do we do now, Head Alpha?" Abby asked me.

I wanted to scream, "I don't know," but I couldn't do that, so I let out a big sigh.

"We need to stop them," Nickoli said so softly I almost didn't hear him.

"What?" someone from the back of the group asked.

"We need to stop them." Nickoli loudly repeated. "You think this did anything to stop them?" No one said anything. "Irene and Roonie." His voice cracked. He cleared his throat and tried again. "Irene and Roonie died for nothing if we don't truly stop them."

"How do we go about that?" I asked. "We can't do this again."

"We take out their leader. Just like we did here. We take out Majie and the damned Appointed fall." He had so much malice in his voice, it scared me for a second. "We need a small targeted attack to get the job done." Evander rejoined the group, signaling that the portal was ready. Nickoli addressed him. "All of my guys need to go home." His tone was stern and left no room for arguing. None of the guys looked like they were going to argue anyway.

Evander nodded, and the boys wordlessly separated from the group to collect their things.

Everyone from my pack volunteered to stay. "No," I told them. "It's too many, and I need you to tell the pack what happened. Send a messenger to the Shilo pack, too. One may stay." They arm-wrestled for the honor, and Deegan won.

"You're going to need some muscle for this, anyway." He gloated and flexed his biceps. I ignored him.

"Everyone else needs to go home," I said to Evander. Addressing the group again, "Hunter, you'll carry Cailyn back. Take her straight to my mother. Abby, you tell the Shilo pack Uncle is no longer in charge. Ethan and Belén, you let the pack know what happened here." They all nodded at their instruction. Cailyn snored from her spot on the ground, out cold from the potion she drank.

I stopped Ethan and Belén before they broke away from the group. "I'll find a way to send word to the pack with updates. If more than a week goes by without hearing from me," I paused. "It'll probably be safe to find a new Head Alpha."

With their belongings in hand, the shifters and the wolves went home.

CHAPTER 40

Nickoli, Deegan, the witches, and I were the only ones left.

Evander finished with the portals and rejoined the group. Alec and Dana circled the clearing, checking everything out, but staying away from the scent of fresh blood.

"Well, I think we all deserve some rest," Evander said.

"Not here," Nickoli mumbled.

"Gods, no!" Evander looked horrified. "You'll come home with us. We can formulate a plan after everyone enjoys a nice lie-down."

That sounded so nice, but we had a task that urgently needed attending before anything else.

I cleared my throat and said, "We need to put them to rest first."

A somber hush fell over the group. I continued, "We can try to bury them or make a pyre..." I trailed off, not sure of these peoples' burial customs.

"There's no way I'm leaving him here," Nickoli said.

"A pyre will be fine," Mabel said softly.

"We need to dig a spot around the pyre so the fire won't spread. The rest of us can go collect wood," I instructed.

Nickoli and Mabel volunteered to dig. Soon we erected twin structures, side by side and ready for burning.

Irene laid on one, and Roonie on the other. Mabel removed a small silver ring from Irene's finger. Roonie wore a thin shell necklace, which Nickoli removed.

Candence reached out and gave Mabel's hand a big squeeze. She let go and stepped up to Irene's pyre. Flames shot out from her fingertips and toward the base of the pyre. It caught quickly, and she moved over to Roonie's. When she finished, she walked back over to Mabel and held her hand. We all stood there for a moment, watching and holding hands with our neighbors.

"These were brave people." I cut in over the crackling sound of the fire. "They did not know what was in store for them, but showed up anyway." I paused. "They will never be forgotten." Nickoli silently wept beside me. I gave his hand the most comforting squeeze I could give. "And we will not let them die in vain," Deegan grumbled out a noise in agreement.

Softly, Evander said, "Grab your things, everyone, we're going home."

CHAPTER 41

While we all grabbed our things, Evander briefly spoke with the vampires. He returned as soon as we each slung our backpacks onto our backs.

"They said they'll keep watch here," Evander informed us. "Fire safety and all that." The two of them stood still as stone. They could have been mistaken for statues by the way the fires cast shadows onto their bodies. "Come on, let's get going."

It took the witches mere moments to shrink their tents and be ready to go. Evander plucked his board from his shirt pocket and tossed it to the ground, enlarging it as it fell; the other witches carried their brooms at the ready.

"Leza," Sage motioned me over, "you can ride with me."

Nickoli already took the place behind Evander; he had clearly done this before. "Okay," I said, trying to control the nervousness in my voice. She sat on the broom with both legs on the same side, so I copied her as I took my place beside her.

"Take your pick, Deegan," I said lightly, trying to relax into the idea of what was about to happen. For a moment, he stood there, unsure of where to go. Candence patted the back end of her broom, inviting him over. He sat down in the same manner, with both legs on the same side, and you could see the whites of his knuckles as he held onto either side of the broom so tightly.

"Hold on tight," Sage said. I circled my arms around her waist, and we lifted off.

We flew into the air together, well above the treetops. My feet dangled, and my head felt dizzy when I glanced down.

I didn't realize I made a sound until Sage said, "It's better if you don't look down."

I looked about and found Nickoli. One hand gripped Evander's shoulder. He didn't seem worried, so I tried to relax. My eyes found Deegan next. He squeezed his eyes shut so tight, the rest of his face scrunched up. I chuckled. At least I was doing better than that.

We took off, smoothly launching toward the northeast. I involuntarily yelped. Sage patted my hand with one of her's in reassurance.

The rush of the air made my eyes water and presented a constant cool breeze on my face. I did my best to look around, except down, but the night sky didn't provide enough light for me to take in my surroundings. The stars whizzed by in streaks. It looked beautiful up here.

◆ ◆ ◆

Soon we spotted some lights on the ground and Sage slowed as we approached. The lights came from tall lanterns stuck in the ground. I saw more vardos than I had ever seen before in my life. They ranged in color from light maple to dark walnut and grouped in circles of no more than ten. A stone path marked the way between all of them. Some even had small twinkling lights strung around them.

"Whoa." I breathed as we came toward it.

"Home sweet home," Sage said, and we touched down outside one of the circles.

Everyone else landed in the same area. They gave goodbye hugs and departed for their homes. That left Sage, Liam, Evander, Nickoli, Deegan, and me standing around.

"Well, that one is mine." Evander pointed to a rosy chestnut-colored vardo on the left side. "I only have one guest room, though, so we're going to have to split you up. Dibs on Nickoli, and I assume that means you too, Leza."

I blushed, and Nickoli said, "Yes."

"Sorry," Evander was addressing Deegan now, "You'll have to sleep up top."

We said good night to Sage and Liam and followed Evander into his home.

In the back was a bed that looked a bit too small for Evander, considering how tall he was. It had two sliding doors to close it off from the rest of the room. There was a wood-burning stove with a set of two cabinets on either side, a small round table set for 2, and a two-seater bench with cushions. Photos adorned the walls, and four lanterns, two on each side, illuminated the space.

"Is this the guest room?" Deegan asked, eyeing the bench, "Where is up top?" He glanced at the ceiling.

"This is the up top part." Evander chuckled. He bent down and pulled at a ring on the floor. A square opened up, revealing a staircase. "We'll be down here. Make yourself comfortable; as you can see, the bed is right there. The bathroom is down the stairs and at the end of the hall." He began his descent.

"Good night, Deegan." I called, following Evander.

It was a relatively short staircase that ended with a short hallway. Light guided our path from recesses in the ceiling. The hallway contained two doors, one on the left and one on the right, as well as two switches on the wall to the left of Evander.

"Bathroom, guest room." Evander pointed to the door at the end of the hall and the door to our right. "We'll get a couple of hours of shut-eye, then I'll make some coffee, and we can regroup. Sound good?"

"Sounds good," I replied, and Nickoli nodded.

Evander called up the stairs to Deegan. "I'm turning off the lights up there but leaving the ones down here on."

"Okay," Deegan called, as we heard his steps walk over toward the bed. Evander flipped one of the switches, and the light from upstairs extinguished.

"Good night," Evander said and pushed open his door.

I grabbed Nickoli's hand and lead him into the guest room, closing the door behind us. When I touched him, I felt his deep sadness.

Instead of a switch, I noticed a slider on the wall. I slid it down, and the lights dimmed with it. I left just enough light to see, and we dropped our bags by the door. Nickoli crawled into bed. His back was to me as I crawled in beside him. I waited a moment before gently turning him to face me. I scooted close and laid his head on my chest. His tears found their way onto my skin. I stroked his hair until we both fell asleep.

CHAPTER 42

A few knocks at the door woke us.

"Coffee is ready," Evander called through the door. "We don't want to waste the day."

We heard his steps recede as he turned and ascended the stairs. "I'm going to use the bathroom; I'll see you upstairs." with that, I leaned over and kissed Nickoli on the shoulder. In our sleep, we must have untangled from each other. Nickoli grumbled something that sounded like an acknowledgment. I picked up my pack and headed toward the bathroom.

The bathroom was smaller than the one at Nickoli's house. It didn't have a basin, just a stall, a toilet, and a sink. Those last two, at least, I knew how to work.

At the mirror, I brushed my hair and secured it into a tight bun, then I brushed my teeth.

I made a mental note to apologize to Evander later. My clothes were covered in filth and had absolutely soiled the sheets. After I finished cleaning up and changing into fresh clothes, I did my best to separate my dirty clothes from my clean belongings when I repacked my bag.

When I exited the bathroom, Nickoli stood waiting outside the door. "I'm going to take a shower." He said. "I won't be long." He gave me a quick kiss on the lips, and energy surged through my body, radiating from the point of contact. His eyes still looked sad, but I think some rest made him feel a bit better.

Not knowing what to do with my bag, I dropped it off in the guest room on my way up the stairs.

Pungent coffee smells greeted my nose as I entered the small cabin area. Four mugs with coffee already poured sat waiting for us on the little round table. A small thing of sugar, milk, and some sort of tincture in an amber glass with a dropper also crowded on the table.

Evander and Deegan sat on the bench. Evander appeared in the middle of some story, while Deegan looked mildly uncomfortable. Relief washed over his face when he saw me.

"Leza, good morning," Deegan said, not caring that he cut off Evander.

"Yes, good morning," Evander said, unphased by the interruption. "Where's Coli?"

"Taking a quick shower."

"Ah, yes, that makes sense. I took one earlier. I'm surprised I didn't wake you two up when I did; made me feel like a brand-new man, though."

I sat at the table and eyed a cup, but didn't want to take one until formally offered. "What were you two talking about?" I asked, just to make conversation.

"Oh, nothing of importance," Evander said. "Just talking about the vardo." He patted the wall affectionately.

"It must be nice to take your home where ever you need to go."

"You know, only a few of us go wheeling and dealing anymore. It's more of a tradition at this point."

"Oh," I said, not knowing how else to respond. I guess I never really thought about how seldom I'd met witches before this.

"Ah, good." Evander said, as he noticed Nickoli emerging from the stairs below. Nickoli took the empty seat by Deegan.

"Cream and sugar, everyone?" We all nodded. Evander put a splash of milk in all the mugs and then stirred in two spoonsful of sugar. Next, he grabbed the tincture bottle and placed a drop in one mug, then handed it to me. He put two drops in two other mugs, then handed one off to Nickoli. He eyed Deegan for a moment. "You're a big boy." He said. "Let's go for three." He put three drops in the last mug and handed it to Deegan.

"What is it?" Deegan asked, looking at his mug suspiciously.

"Old family recipe," Evander said, and took a sip. He shimmed his shoulders in delight. "It will make you feel right as rain, and after last night, I think we all need it."

Nickoli took a big gulp, and his shoulders relaxed. I followed suit. Deegan took his sip last.

I immediately felt like I just woken up from the best sleep of my life, which felt strange considering I couldn't have slept for more than a couple of hours. "This stuff is amazing." I marveled aloud. Evander just winked. Embarrassingly enough, my stomach growled right at that moment. The coffee must have woken it up, too.

Evander laughed. "Sage invited us over for breakfast. If you'll bring your mugs and follow me." He led us out and across to a pale blue vardo. Little carved birds decorated the wood by the door. Evander knocked, but didn't wait for a reply before opening the door. The inside had a similar setup to Evander's, even the little door hiding stairs in the middle of the cabin. Evander made his way directly down them, calling out, "Sis, we're starving."

"Then come to the kitchen," Sage called from below us.

The stairs ended again in a hallway, but here Sage's had more doors, some open and some not. Our noses led us to one of the open doors which contained the kitchen. It resembled Nickoli's with some similar equipment, but wasn't as big, housing only a few pale blue counters with white tops, an apparatus for cooking, and something to store the food in. A square table with four chairs waited for us in the right corner of the room. Even though the space had no windows, it still seemed as if fresh morning light filled the room.

Sage and Liam carried over big plates of scrambled eggs and toast to the table.

"Moring," Sage greeted as she sat the food down. Liam mimicked her. With their hands now free, they each grabbed hold of a corner of the table and gave a coordinated yank. The table grew in length by several inches. Liam took a chair and split it in two, making a copy. He sat it down and did the same thing on the side with another chair, bringing the total number of chairs to six, one for each of us. Sage brought over a stack of plates and cups while Liam fetched a handful of forks.

"Sit, sit." She instructed, and we didn't argue.

Nickoli, myself, and Deegan took the three seats situated on the outside, facing the hall. That left the three inward-facing seats for Sage, Liam, and Evander to arrange themselves.

One by one, we filled our plates and began eating. In no time at all, we finished and returned to sipping our coffees.

"That was delicious," Evander stated.

I was ready to agree when Deegan opened his dumb mouth. "How are we going to eliminate the threat?" A gloom settled over the room, and I elbowed him. "Ow, what?"

Evander sighed. "I guess we should get to it."

Wordlessly, Sage and Liam excused themselves from the table and started cleaning up.

"With how small our group is, sneaking in is our best option," Deegan offered.

"How big is the place?" Evander asked.

"I don't really know," I answered. I didn't get to see much of it before we escaped, and it wasn't in the headspace to make a mental map on the way out." I looked over at Nickoli for him to pick up the conversation.

"Big." He said. "They have sentries setup as well, but it's not well coordinated."

"That sounds promising," Evander said.

"Then we target their leader," Deegan said. "This Majie lady, how hard will it be to reach her?"

"I know where her room is if that's what you're asking, but it's guaranteed to be warded."

"That's why I'm going, remember?" Evander interjected. "I can, at the very least, sense wards. At the very most, I can undo them."

Remembering how she knocked me around when we first met, I blurted out, "She can defend herself too, and easily."

Deegan sat back and thought for a moment. "What are some good long-range and short-range attack options?"

"We can poison her," Nickoli said quietly. We all looked at him. "There's a plethora of delivery methods. We could taint a weapon, get it into the air, put it into a drink."

Evander perked up. "I like that idea! We could even try all of them." Deegan and I nodded in agreement. "I know exactly who we need to see."

CHAPTER 43

Evander led us down a path leading away from the bulk of the vardos. We approached an enormous structure made entirely of glass. Fog gathered at the top and condensation dripped down the outside of the glass.

"What are we doing here?" Deegan asked.

"If we want good reliable poison, then we need to talk to Bramble," Evander said as if that explained everything. "Bramble is our resident plant expert, which means they'll know exactly what kind of toxins we need to get the job done." Evander gave a light rap on the glass door. Their surroundings resembled a jungle. Rows and rows of different plants crowded together. Directly inside the door was a small discernable path, but that was quickly swallowed up by large overhanging leaves.

The leaves shimmied as someone approached to answer the door.

When the someone answered the door, their big round glasses immediately fogged over. An alabaster hand removed them and began cleaning the glass, using the tan apron they wore around their waist. Their choppy hair fell to their chin. It looked as if they just cut off any part of their hair that gets in their way. I stood at least a head taller than them, and they sported a slim build. Their face had very angular features smudged with dirt. Their small hands worked quickly at the glasses before placing them back on their face, making their hazel eyes bulge from their face.

"Bramble." Evander greeted, "How's it going?"

Bramble blinked up at Evander several times before a too-big of a grin spread across their face. 'Evander!" Bramble exclaimed in a high tenor voice. "Come in, come in!" They ushered us inside without proper introductions. A sad look crossed over Bramble's face. "I still haven't unlocked the secrets of crossing a rose with a venus flytrap."

"I'm sure you'll get there," Evander said reassuringly.

The interior of the glass structure felt uncomfortably hot. A sheen of sweat formed quickly on my exposed arms. Bramble seemed to notice us as if for the first time and dug around in their apron pocket. "Who are your friends?" They asked, pulling out a small, empty and transparent container with a wide opening at the top. Evander introduced everyone as Bramble quickly swiped the container up my arm, collecting the sweat. I jumped back. Bramble didn't seem to notice. He produced a cork from another pocket and sealed the jar of sweat. "You'll never know what will end up being useful," Bramble said, and tucked the sweat jar in a third pocket. Bramble stuck out their hand for a shake. I looked over at Evander, giving him a concerned look. He didn't look bothered at all, so I hesitantly took Bramble's hand. Bramble's fingers looked best suited for flute playing, but possessed a surprising strength. Bramble also shook with Nickoli and Deegan.

"What can Bramble do for you?"

"Well," Began Evander, "we need your help with something rather unsavory, but you're the most qualified to help us."

"Mhm," Bramble said, and started making their way back down the path of plants. Evander hurried to catch up, and we followed.

"We need something deadly," Evander explained.

Bramble's eyes sparkled. "How deadly?"

"No chance the target can get away, deadly."

While they conversed, Deegan inspected a pretty pink five-lobed funnel-shaped flower. He reached toward it when Bramble casually said, "Don't touch that."

Instinctually, I reached out and smacked Deegan's hand away from the plant. I don't need anyone falling out in here, and if someone was gleeful at the prospect of procuring something deadly, then I knew to listen when they instruct not to touch something.

"When do you need this by?" Bramble asked as he pivoted to the left. Tucked away at the end of the path sat a worktable that held several bowls, strainers, leaves, roots, containers, and a very large mortar and pestle. Bramble started organizing the things on the table to make room.

"No later than sunset," Evander answered. Bramble ran toward and grabbed a pot of the plant Deegan almost touched, and brought it back to the table.

"No problem," Bramble stated, practically chuckling with glee.

"We will leave you to it, then," Evander said, ushering us back toward the door. Bramble didn't acknowledge him and ran off deeper into the glasshouse.

Once outside, the fresh air provided tremendous relief. "Well. That was something." I said.

"Bramble is the best botanist I've ever known. We'll get exactly what we want, trust me."

CHAPTER 44

My anxiety grew as we waited for Bramble to finish, but I had no choice but to put my faith in their work. We all waited back at Evander's. Nickoli showed me how to work the shower, and after I finished up, I instructed Deegan. Evander was right; the shower made me feel like a brand-new person.

We lounged in the cabin part of Evander's vardo for a while. Nickoli and I sat at the bench while Deegan sprawled across the bed and Evander sat at the little table.

Evander helped pass the time by telling us stories of past witches. It astounded me to learn these people could accomplish anything they set their minds to while utilizing little physical effort. To lift a boulder, they simply had to think about it or wave their hand around. For us to lift the same boulder, we would have to work day in and day out to build up our strength.

Deegan relaxed a little as he told stories of our pack and its past. He had never mingled with outsiders before, and you could tell he was unsure of how to conduct himself.

For lunch, Sage, Liam, Candence, and even Mabel joined us for a picnic. Evander led us outside, to see everything already set up, and everyone already waiting. Mabel wore black from head to toe in mourning, but politely engaged with us. Sage pulled everything from a large enchanted basket. At least three different types of sandwiches were piled high on a giant platter.

They set up pitchers of water and juices for everyone to pick from. Candence brought a platter of soft lemon lavender cookies.

The afternoon passed surprisingly lovely, despite the preceding events and what we still had coming.

CHAPTER 45

When the sun set on the horizon, Evander rounded us up, and we headed back toward the glass structure.

Tall lamps flickered on by themselves as darkness settled in. Many of the vardos were lit from the inside, and some jostled as their inhabitants moved around.

The sense of community here reminded me of my pack, and I smiled to myself.

The door flung open as we approached.

"Fellows!" Bramble exclaimed. "You have exquisite timing; I was just about to fetch you." Bramble enthusiastically flapped their hands, motioning us to come in. Bramble vibrated with excitement as they led us back to the worktable. On the table rested two containers. Both containers held a noxious, green-colored substance, one powder, and the other a liquid.

"Well, what do we have here?" Evander asked.

"Only death in a bottle!" The glee in Bramble's voice as they said those words disturbed me. "I've combined toxins from the world's most dangerous plants." From one of the many pockets on Bramble's apron, they produced pairs of gloves. "If you put these on, you can handle the powder and throw it in someone's face, but, under no circumstance should you touch your own face after you've handled the powder. It's safest to burn the gloves after use." Bramble reflected, then carried on. "You can dip weapons into the liquid. One knick, and it'll do the trick!"

"You're positive?" I asked.

"Deadly serious." Bramble cackled.

"Well, Bramble, I dare say you've exceeded any expectation I had," Evander said, gingerly picking up the containers and taking the gloves from Bramble. Evander handed us each a pair to hang on to.

"My pleasure. It's so nice to be challenged!"

"Pending we survive this ordeal," Evander said, bringing a somber mood to the group. "Come see me if you need anything. I'll be sure you'll get it."

Bramble's eyes twinkled. "With that stuff," Bramble pointed one of their long fingers at the containers, "you're sure to survive!"

We all muttered our thanks and goodbyes before walking back to Evander's vardo in silence.

◆ ◆ ◆

"Alright," Evander said abruptly, startling me. "Let's get a good night's sleep and trek off in the morning, yeah? The sooner we get this over with, the better." Evander opened up his door, and we all filed in.

"Sounds like a plan!" Deegan said with more enthusiasm than I had heard from him all day. At least one of us was excited. He nestled into the little bed and hollered a "good night" as Evander, Nickoli, and I descended the stairs.

"Uh, Evander." I stopped before he broke away from us. "Do you have an extra set of sheets? I didn't realize how dirty we were before we slept in bed. I'd like a clean set."

Evander waved his hand. "Don't even worry about it; it's all already taken care of."

"Thank you."

"Besides," He continued, "you'll just dirty them up again." He winked and quickly closed the door behind him. Nickoli's cheeks burned.

CHAPTER 46

I suspect Evander must have cast some sort of relaxation spell because I slept uncharacteristically well, considering what today had in store for us.

Nickoli and I made sure we didn't forget any of our things, then made our way upstairs. Deegan sat waiting, all packed up and waiting for us.

"About time." He teased, way too excited.

"Shut up." I scolded. My tone must have sounded frightening because he shrank back. "You have no idea what Majie is like or the power she holds." Nickoli's eyes went dark, and I knew he felt the same. "We have to be precise and extraordinarily careful." I paused. "We want to come back from this."

"Well, that's the freaking spirit, isn't it?" Evander said as he climbed the stairs.

Nickoli glared at him. "We don't need to mess around."

"I know, but we could have a little confidence. Goes a long way, you know." Evander wore a large leather satchel at his side and absently patted it. He must have Bramble's death in a bottle tucked away in there. "Everyone got their gloves?" We all nodded. "Good. So, what's the plan?" He looked pointedly at me.

I gulped. Everyone's eyes turned to me. I fought back the urge to shriek and run away. *Get a hold of yourself!* My inner voice scolded. *This is what it means to be Head Alpha. This is the role you have dreamed about for practically your whole life.* I set my jaw, squared my shoulders, and addressed them. "We need to get there unnoticed."

"We could portal there." Evander offered.

I shook my head. "We don't know if there are any patrols, and we don't need to appear in front of anyone."

Nickoli cleared his throat. "That tunnel I made when we escaped should still be there. All we'd have to do is unseal the entrance."

I thought for a moment. I couldn't think of a better entry point, so I agreed. "Deegan and I can take point together. We should be able to hear or smell anyone patrolling around." Deagan nodded enthusiastically.

"That settles it," Evander said. "We'll portal to the tunnel, and then it's show time." He said this calmly enough, but beads of sweat developed on his forehead.

CHAPTER 47

Our escape tunnel looked exactly as it did when we left; circular slabs laid out like knocked-over dominos.

Deegan forcefully eyed the ground. "There are only two sets of tracks around. No one but you two have been here."

I felt a small amount of relief, and my shoulders fell. "Good." I said aloud to everyone, "That means they never followed us out and won't know we are coming." This was our best chance. "Deegan, to my right, please." He obeyed without a word, but seemed to hum with energy. "Nickoli in the middle and Evander in the rear." They fell into position.

"Before we begin." Evander piped up. "I took the liberty of divvying up our secret weapon." He flipped open the flap to his satchel and handed us each a cloth baggie of powder and a small glass vial of liquid. Deegan hesitated before taking his. "Don't worry," Evander reassured. "I've charmed these to be tough as stone, so nothing should puncture or break them. Perfectly safe. Tuck it in your pocket and forget it's there for now." Evander smiled at us, but his eyes looked wild with fear.

I cleared my throat to grab their attention. I placed the baggie in my left pocket and the vial in my right. "As you said, show time." I took a step forward, leading my team into the tunnel.

We remained quiet, but quick. Evander produced a small orb of light that bobbed just in front of me, so the terrain wouldn't slow us down. Nickoli briefly took the lead when it came time to open the other side. As soon as light penetrated the tunnel, Evander's orb went out. The rock slab boomed as it hit the ground, and we froze, listening intently. After some time, we didn't hear any commotion, so we took it as our cue to move.

"This way," Nickoli said before shifting into a falcon. We followed. Deegan and I side by side and Evander behind us. My ears strained to hear every little thing I could. A deer galloped in the west, some birds high in the trees fiddled with twigs as they built their nests, and a squirrel scurried not far off, but no footsteps.

When we neared the camp, Nickoli reverted into human form and stood in front of Evander.

Electricity filled the air, fueled by the group's collective nerves. I could only pick up on five sets of footprints roaming the nearby area. Other than that, the quiet was overwhelming. I couldn't focus on that right now, but the lack of movement unsettled me.

"Nickoli," I whispered. "Where does she live?"

"It's a sturdy oak structure. We are going to have to move inside a little." He gestured to the few buildings we could see. "But if you circle around to the left, you'll know it when you see it."

I looked at him, confused.

"It will all make sense when we're in there."

I nodded curtly and resolutely said, "Alright."

Everyone looked at me with palpable anxiety. I took a moment to return each of their looks, hoping I conveyed some kind of confidence.

Deegan stilled in an expert show of concentration. "I follow you, Head Alpha." My heart raced at my new title.

Evander set his brow. "We've got a good plan." He sounded like he was reassuring himself more than trying to reassure us.

Nickoli held my gaze and didn't say a word. He closed the small distance between us in a few quick steps, stopping with his lips on mine before I could form any words. The colors erupted. His kiss was fierce, but short. When he pulled back, the colors pulled back as if sucked down a drain. I wanted to fling my body onto his. I decided I would not die here today so I could still have a chance of giving into that temptation some other day.

"Save it for the victory party," Evander said, and chuckled shakily.

I rolled my eyes at him and whispered, "Let's go."

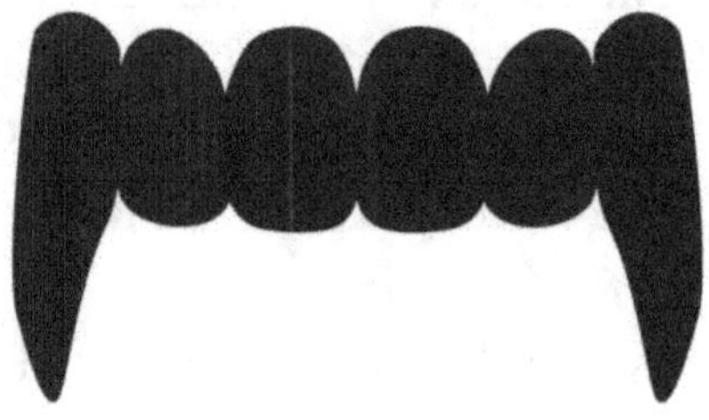

CHAPTER 48

André

Reverently, André slipped the portrait of Maria into a silk drawstring bag and cinched it shut. He walked over toward the hanging curtains and ripped one down with minimal effort. He used the fabric to give Maria's bag extra padding.

He placed his forehead against its cushioned surface and closed his eyes. "Pas pour longtemps." He whispered, continuing to hold the portrait close to him for a moment longer before placing it at the top of a very packed trunk. He closed the lid and whined when he had to use more force than he'd like to latch the lid closed. The portrait should be safe, but he didn't want to take any chances with it.

André had decided to leave. It was full daylight now, and his coffin stood open, beckoning him to enter. As tired as he felt, he refused its summons. Majie knew how much he hated being awake at this unnatural hour, so she wouldn't expect him to be up, making it a perfect time to get away.

A large piece of dark grey fabric laid on top of the coffee table next to a rectangular wooden box. Andre draped the fabric around him and fastened it into a cloak with a simple silver pin. The hood pooled around his face, casting it into a shadow. The ends lightly touched the ground, covering him from head to toe. After what happened last time, he couldn't risk the protection spell shorting out. If worst came to worst, he could hunker down, and the cloak could shield him from the sunlight.

He frowned at the rectangular box before placing it on top of the trunk. He scooped up the trunk and situated it under his arm and against his hip as if it weighed nothing. Without a second look back, he ascended the stairs and stopped at the door. With his free hand, he swiftly popped open the box and removed an amulet. He was told this is what Americans call a quarter, a coin currency for them. He slipped it into his breast pocket, and the spell washed over him in a translucent shimmer.

A noise caught his attention as he reached for the door. He heard a group walking around outside. He couldn't risk any witnesses. Annoyed, he waited them out, but a particular heartbeat kept grabbing his attention. He set the trunk down and pushed it against the wall so he had room to open the door and peek out. He quickly realized this was useless. All he could see was straight ahead to Majie's. Two factors prevented him from opening the door further. The first being, it would alert the group to his presence, and he didn't want that. Second, the trunk sat in the way. He couldn't open the door much wider anyway, just enough to wedge himself out. He used all of his might to strain his vision to see who it was, but couldn't and had to close the door again to avoid revealing himself.

He pressed himself against the door and listened intently, focusing on the familiar heartbeat. Soon after, realization spread through him like a flame on dry grass. "La fillette." He mouthed to himself. What is she doing here? André honestly hadn't even given the little werewolf girl a second thought since she escaped with Majie's pet bird. That is how much Majie had angered him.

André continued to listen as the group passed by. Based on their direction, it only made sense they intended for Majie's place. He counted time with their heartbeats. They should have made it to Majie's by now. He heard a bang shortly followed by a door slamming shut. André opened the door to peek out once more. No one. He unfastened his cloak and dropped it to the floor. The protection spell had just activated, so André wasn't concerned about burning in the sun. He wedged himself out the door and closed it behind him. Taking long strides, he crossed the short distance to Majie's in no time and slunk around the back, where he knew there would be a window.

CHAPTER 49

Leza

My heart raced as we hurried through The Appointed's encampment. No one roamed about, and we hadn't come across any sentries. Was this good or bad for us? Had there been people milling about when Nickoli and I escaped? I couldn't remember. They chased us, yes, but that isn't the same as a typical day in the encampment.

I shook my head to clear my thoughts. "*Focus!*" I commanded myself. "*Worry about people when or if you come across them. For now, the important part is getting to Majie's.*"

Nickoli had been right. I knew Majie's place when I saw it. I assume the structures we passed by were all dwellings of some sort, and they looked like they thrown together. Not this one, though. They constructed this one out of oak timber, and it carried an official and authoritative air with it.

We crossed diagonally through some walkways to shorten the distance to her door, and I picked up my speed to a jog.

My mind panicked. "*What if she had wards?*" Why hadn't I thought about that sooner? It's only natural that a witch would lay wards around her home. Too late to worry about that now.

I braced myself and shouldered open the door, violently swinging it inward. Nothing happened. No instant death, no searing pain, no zap of any kind.

My group rushed in behind me.

"That was stupid!" Evander hissed at me.

The place was empty.

This structure only had one room, no bigger than my hut back home. The walls were just exposed oak timber and packed dirt made up the floor. Only two pieces of furniture sat in the room. The first, a simple mattress pushed against the left wall, adorned only by a thin sheet and one plump pillow, both neutral in color.

The other piece of furniture was a large, sturdy altar separated into two shelves. The smaller top shelf displayed a gleaming sharp knife with a long hilt made from bone. The blade itself appeared a foot long. The larger bottom contained vials, piles of loose herbs, and several colored candles. A small window, halfway up the length of the wall, separated the two furniture pieces.

The door slammed shut behind us, causing me to jump. We all whirled around to discover Majie standing in the previously empty doorway.

"What are you doing?" Her voice boomed in my head, making my ears ring from the inside.

Nickoli wasted no time rushing her, quietly and quickly, but no match for her. She calmly looked in his direction as he charged and flung him away with an invisible force, as if he were nothing more than a gnat. Nickoli slammed into the wall behind him and crumpled down onto the floor. He didn't get up, but I could see his chest rise and fall as he breathed.

Evander tensed his fingers with purpose, but nothing happened. He vigorously shook his hands, then tried the purposeful tensing again. Nothing. Panicked, he looked over at me. What was I supposed to do?

Majie let out a visceral laugh, and she fizzled from sight. Evander crept toward the once again empty door. I heard Majie set her hands down on the altar behind us. Deegan and I whirled again to face her. In a show of arrogance, she faced away from us, shifting things around on the altar in front of her, unconcerned with us.

I chanced a glance at Deegan and noticed him pouring some of Bramble's power into his gloved hand. He started edging closer and closer to her. What could she possibly be doing? She wasn't even picking things up, just scootching them around.

I heard Deegan inhale deeply, then he carefully brought his hand up to his face. Majie spun and faced him. He puffed out his pent-up air, and powder shot straight into her face. Deegan scrambled backward to avoid any lingering powder in the air.

Majie didn't even blink. She gestured her hand out, palm facing up, fingers splayed and cackled. "Poison?" She mused. "That was your big plan?"

I tried to take a step back but couldn't; then, I noticed the air trapped in my throat. I couldn't breathe. The only part of me that could move was my eyes. I couldn't see Deegan and Evander from where I stood, but I didn't hear them move, so I assumed they couldn't move as well. My eyes shot back to Majie in horror as it dawned on me what was happening.

Majie laughed heartily, the tinkling sound mixing with the ringing still in my ears. "Hadn't you considered for a moment that someone may have already tried this before and failed?" She chastised. As she spoke, pale hands appeared on the window and slowly started lifting the glass.

"Foolish children." She tsked in a mock tone of scolding. The long fingers of hands gripping the window curled under the glass to guide it the rest of the way up. My lungs burned. "You annoy me." Her voice dripped with malice. "But in a few moments, you won't be annoying me anymore." She smirked, missing the face standing at the window, which belonged to the vampire that marked me. The edges of my vision darkened.

The vampire entered the room, silent as a cat. He grabbed the hilt of the knife displayed on the altar, then moved too fast for my eyes to follow. In the next instant, the point of the blade greeted our eyes from Majie's chest, piercing her heart. I greedily sucked air into my lungs. Evander and Deegan coughed and sputtered around me.

Majie looked down in genuine disbelief as a dark red stain seeped rapidly into the fabric of her white dress.

I noticed Nickoli stir from where he lay, and I rushed over to protect him. He groaned and rubbed his head as he came to.

Evander produced sparks from the ends of his fingers. His magic had returned! He readied a fireball to throw, with Deegan poised, ready to pounce beside him.

Majie turned her head to look at her assailant in shock. A black, bile-like substance leaked from the corner of her mouth. She sank to her knees and slumped to the floor. As the life left her body, her skin aged and shriveled, and her silvery, white hair fell out in chunks. Nothing remained but the husk of an ancient woman.

Before Evander or Deegan could initiate their attack, the vampire spoke on his way back to the open window. "I am leaving for the mainlands." He kept his eyes on Evander and the fire. "This place is no longer any concern of mine." In a flash, he exited through the window.

CHAPTER 50

D eegan and Evander exchanged a confused glance while the fireball in Evander's palm extinguished. Evander rummaged around in his satchel as he approached Nickoli and me. "Bonked your head pretty good, huh?" He asked as he squatted down to get on Nickoli's level.

"Yeah," Nickoli replied.

Evander fished out a bottle and shook out two oval-shaped pills with white and blue swirls in them. He handed them over to Nickoli, saying, "Here, take these." Nickoli obediently popped them into his mouth. "It'll fix you right up." I passed Nickoli my canteen so he could wash the pills down. "And, they're almost fully tested." Nickoli narrowed his eyes at him, cheeks full of water. "I joke! They're fine." Nickoli swallowed and handed me back my canteen. His shoulders fell, and he stopped rubbing at his head.

Deegan cleared his throat, and we turned to look at him. He held out his entire supply of poison to Evander. He had already removed the gloves and inverted the cloth to encompass both containers. "I really don't want these anymore." His brows knitted together, and he clearly looked uncomfortable.

"Come to think of it, I don't want mine either," I said, mimicking Deegan. The vials gave off an unruly aura that made me uncomfortable to be around—probably due to how deadly

Bramble stressed these substances were. It's the same uneasiness I have around venomous snakes and poisonous berries.

Evander collected all of our vials and pouches and tucked them back into his satchel. He mused aloud to himself, "Bramble will be most perplexed that this didn't work. They were so sure of themselves."

Nickoli made to get up, but I impulsively threw myself at him, wrapping my arms around his neck and making him sit back down again. "It's over!" I exclaimed and let the wonderful colors fill the room, exhilarated by the fact we all survived. I let go of Nickoli and stood up with him. Evander rose along with us.

"Is it over?" Deegan asked. "There's something going on outside."

I paused to listen. He was right. A man's voice presented some sort of speech outside. "Let's go check it out," I said, making my way to the door. The boys filed out behind me. I swung open the door and saw way more people than I had expected. Especially considering how deserted it appeared on our way in. At least thirty people now filled the yard. With Majie's spells now broken, most of the people in the yard walked around groggily, as if they had just woken up from a dream.

I saw that vampire again and he was the one speaking. He stood atop a trunk and had a dark grey cloak draped around him. He spied me and wrapped up his speech. "I'm leaving this place. I'm tired of waiting around on this stupid island. I'm going back to the mainlands and taking the fight to where the battle actually is." He dismounted from his makeshift pedestal. "To kill humans." He spat out the last word as if the word itself tasted foul in his mouth. With ease, he picked the trunk up, tucked it up under one arm, then started walking away. A handful of people departed from the group to follow him.

I cleared my throat, and the group of still mostly sleepy people looked my way. "Majie is dead." I projected my voice, trying to make the whole encampment hear me. "This island will no longer tolerate the hate of The Appointed. Either make peace with the fact that while here, the humans on the mainlands hold nothing over us or follow him out." I point in the direction the vampire had headed. A couple more people turned to follow him. "Spread the word," I commanded. "Everyone else is free to go home." I turned, leading my group away from that wretched place.

CHAPTER 51

With the encampment sufficiently behind us, Evander created a portal for us, and we materialized on the other side in Nickoli's backyard. For a moment, I was confused. We needed to go home. Why were we here? And then it hit me. Nickoli had a different home. My heart thumped loudly in my chest. With wide eyes, I turned to look at Nickoli. "I–" I started, but didn't know how to continue. Searching for the words, I looked over at Deegan. "I have to go home." I finally said, turning back to Nickoli. "I have to go home," I repeated.

"I know." He said, his brows furrowed.

"I don't–" Tears welled in my eyes, "want to leave you."

He firmly placed his hands on my shoulders. The tears cast prisms within the colors. "Then don't." He said simply.

"I can't ask you–"

He cut me off. "You didn't." He pulls me into an embrace. "I'm sticking with you."

The tears spilled from my eyes in a state of ataraxia. He squeezed me hard, then let me go. I looked at his house. "But what about your family? Your mom?"

"It's not like I'll never see them again." He reassured me. "I'll come visit them. Besides," He looked over at Evander, "he can enchant some more notebooks or come up with something for us to stay in contact. Right?"

Evander's face held a soft expression, like a mother watching her daughter walk down the aisle on her wedding day. "Of course."

Nickoli rolled his eyes at him. "Come on." He said to me and grabbed my hand. "Let's go tell Mama." The colors descended over my view in easy bliss as he led me inside.

THANK YOU FOR READING!

You've made it to the end of my story. I hope you liked it. Wheather you loved it or hated it (I hope you didn't hate it!), please don't forget to leave a review in order to help more readers discover this book.

Reviews can be left where the book was purchased, on Amazon, and on GoodReads.

GIVING BACK

Ten percent of proceeds goes to support Wolf Concervation Center.

WCC is crucial in preserving Mexican Grey wolves (lobos) and Red wolves.

WCC's mission is to advance the survival of wolves through education, advocacy, research, and recovery.

ABOUT THE AUTHOR

Rachael Balke

Rachael made her publishing debut in 2023.
She was born in Dallas, Texas, then moved to middle Tennessee to be closer to family. She was raised all over middle Tennessee with her formative years spent in Manchester and her adolescent years were spent in Hendersonville.
Rachael has loved writing and reading ever since she was a little girl. She started writing short stories in the second grade, then in high school she took her first creative writing class. As she grew older she continued to write in her free time (even though it feels like free time dries up when you're a grown up).
Her love of writing was reignited when she joined a creative writing class put on by her local library.
Rachael was awarded an honorable mention in the 2022 NYC

Midnight Microfiction Writing contest and can't wait to see
where her writing takes her next!
When she isn't writing, Rachael enjoys playing videogames,
doing arts and crafts, hanging out with her husband, and loving
on her two kitty cats.